Kozart

J. NATHAN

Happy Reading,
Shannon!
I hope you fall
in love with
Kozart!
♡ Natha

Edited by Stephanie Elliot & Gem's Precise Proofreads

Cover Design by Tiffany at T.E. Black Designs
Cover Photo by Eric Battershell
Cover Model Kaz Vanderwaard

First Edition July 2019
ISBN: 9781073583119

For my aspiring writer/detective.
May you always smile, laugh, and be the
best version of you that you can be.
I love you more than the universe.

CHAPTER ONE

Kozart

I checked the clock on the nightstand of my hotel room—the biggest one in the penthouse. It was just after midnight. I glanced at the two sleeping blondes tangled up in my sheets. I'd clearly tired them out. Too bad the same hadn't worked for me.

What the hell was I gonna do now? I certainly didn't want to be there when the two of them woke up—though round two might do the trick and knock my ass out for a change. If it didn't, I was stuck making small talk with girls who wanted nothing more than to brag to their friends that they'd banged a rock star.

I climbed out of bed, collecting my boxers and jeans that had been strewn around the room by the all-too-eager groupies in my bed. I pulled them on, then tugged my black hoodie over my head. I looked around for my ball cap, snatching it off the dresser and pulling it low on my head before venturing out into the living room.

Music blared and bottles covered the surface of the tables. My bandmates drank with other scantily-clad groupies scattered around the massive room. The guys loved the nightly attention they received for being part of the highest grossing band in the world.

"What's up, Z?" my drummer Treyton called over the bass pounding through the room.

The groupies' attention shot to me, their eyes widening on contact. I could almost hear their strategizing thoughts. The stories they'd share with their friends. The relics they planned to steal to commemorate the night they partied with rock stars.

No thanks.

"I'll be back," I called to Treyton.

I slipped out the door and headed for the elevator, hoping no one followed me.

I needed to fucking breathe.

The attention had begun to suffocate me. Probably because the reason behind the attention—the only reason these girls were there falling at our feet—was superficial. And as much as these girls thought they knew us from our music, they didn't know us at all. And even though we might've acted like we wanted to know them in the heat of the moment, we didn't. We'd be on to a whole new town and a whole new slew of girls waiting to take their places.

Once the elevator arrived, I stood alone inside staring at my reflection in the mirrored walls. I'd aged a lot over the past five years. Traveling, partying, and lack of sleep did that to a person. I wondered if all twenty-five-year-olds felt like me. I also wondered when this lifestyle would finally take its toll on me.

Had it already taken its toll?

Because it was beginning to feel a hell of a lot like it had.

CHAPTER TWO

Aubrey

I knew how I looked, face down on the cold marble bar in the ritzy hotel—in a sparkly pink bridesmaid dress no less. But I didn't care. About that. About the pretzel pieces that had gathered in my dark curls spread out over the bar top. About anything.

"You okay?" a deep voice asked from beside me.

"Fine," I grumbled.

"You don't look fine."

My head shot up, a wave of dizziness accompanying the quick movement. "The universal response to seeing someone passed out on a bar is to leave them alone," I informed the guy in the dark hoodie who sat on the stool beside me.

"You're not passed out," he pointed out.

"Doesn't matter. It's how it looks," I said, unable to discern the color of his hair or eyes since both were cloaked in the shade of the dark ball cap pulled low on his head.

He shrugged. "Sorry. Just wanted to make sure you were okay."

I scanned the bar, the hum of conversation suddenly returning to my frazzled brain. "Wow." A humorless laugh escaped me. "You're the only person in this place who even thought to check if I was okay."

He lifted his bottle of beer to his mouth and tipped it back.

"I'm even more pathetic than I thought," I mumbled.

"I thought you just said the universal response was to leave you alone?"

Ignoring his sarcasm, I motioned for the bartender to bring me another of whatever it was I'd been drinking.

"You think that's a good idea?" the guy beside me asked.

I turned to him. "With the night I'm having? Definitely."

He chuckled, the soft rumble tumbling out of him as he reached toward my face and picked a piece of pretzel out of my loose waves. "You got a name?"

"It'd be really weird if I didn't," I sassed.

He chuckled again, this time showing straight white teeth. "You're a feisty drunk."

"I'm not drunk. Just humiliated."

The bartender placed a blue drink down in front of me. I pulled it close and sipped through the skinny red straw. I wasn't lying when I said I wasn't drunk. But I was definitely on my way to getting there.

"What happened?" the guy asked.

I glanced down at my dress flowing down to my open-toed sparkly heels. "My sister just got married."

"Is she younger or something?" he asked.

I glared at him. "You think I'm sulking in a bar because I'm jealous of my sister's happiness?"

He shrugged. "Don't know. Don't know you."

"I'll have you know, I'm a hell of a sister, and a hell of a catch."

"I'm sure you are. I just wouldn't mention 'Passes out in bars' on any dating site profiles. Might not be the clientele you're looking to attract."

My eyes widened. "Dating sites?"

"Yeah. Isn't that what people are doing these days?"

"These days? What are you, sixty?"

He snickered, clearly not much older than me.

"So, if *you're* not doing what people are doing *these days*, are you married?" I asked.

"Nope."

"Divorced?"

He shook his head, seemingly amused.

"Girlfriend?"

He shook his head.

"Boyfriend?"

Laughter burst out of him.

I wanted to question his reaction, but the sound of his amusement made me forget for a couple seconds why I was in the bar alone in the first place.

"You're funny." He lifted his bottle to his smiling lips and downed the rest of his beer.

"I'll add that to my profile."

His eyes cut to mine, and he stared at me long and hard. "What's your name?"

"What's yours?"

"My friends call me Kozart."

I cocked my head. "We're not friends."

He mimicked my cocked head. "We could be."

I scrunched my nose. "Is that a line?"

"Definitely not a line."

"Why? You don't pick up funny bridesmaids passed out in bars?"

He threw back his head and laughed again. "Tell me your name."

I gasped, my head dropping to the top of the bar and my forehead pressing to the sticky cold surface, nearly knocking over my drink.

"What are you doing?" he asked.

"*Shhhhhh.* Pretend I'm not here."

"That's kinda difficult to do."

I said nothing, just stayed in that position. "Is he gone?"

"Who?"

I lifted my head a couple of inches and peeked across the bar to the elevator doors beyond it. They were closed and no one stood in front of them. I lifted my head back up.

"What was that about?" Kozart asked.

"Just avoiding some people."

"I'd say."

I leaned forward and sipped my drink, needing the alcohol more than ever.

"So, is the wedding still going on?" he asked.

"Yup."

"You don't want to be there?"

I shook my head.

"You gonna tell me why you were humiliated."

"I came with a date and left alone."

Kozart's brows shot up. "He dumped you at your sister's wedding?"

"I walked in on him screwing another bridesmaid in the bridal suite." I didn't mean to be so blunt—okay maybe I did. My heart had been stomped on then shattered into a million little embarrassing pieces for good measure.

"Ouch."

"Yup."

A long silence passed between us as I sipped my drink.

"You don't need a douchebag like him anyway," Kozart assured me.

"You have to say that," I said, knowing I hadn't really given him anything else he could've said.

"Babe, I don't say anything I don't wanna say." He dug his hand into his jeans pocket and pulled out a fifty-dollar bill, tossing it onto the bar. "Come on," he said, stepping off his stool. "Take me to the wedding."

I scoffed.

"I'm serious."

"The entire wedding knows what happened."

"Yeah. Some asshole blew his shot with you. *You* did nothing wrong. And now you've got an even better date."

My eyes swept over his black hoodie, faded jeans, and sneakers.

"Not up to par?" he asked.

"Why are you being so nice to me?"

"Because pretty girls should not be passed out in bars when their sister's wedding is going on."

"You called me pretty."

"I did."

"Can I add that to my dating profile?"

He smirked.

I hopped down from my stool, steadying myself on the back of it. Apparently, I drank a bit more than I realized.

Kozart scanned the area around us. "Which way?"

I pointed toward the ballroom. "You sure about this?"

He linked his fingers through mine, catching me completely off guard. His fingers were soft, his grip strong. "Absolutely."

Dance music poured out of the ballroom as we neared. Flashing lights spilled onto the carpet outside the double doors.

I drew a deep breath and donned a smile as he led me into the room.

Groups and couples filled the dance floor, moving to the beat of an old-school hip-hop song I'd loved in junior high—before I became such a country music fan.

Kozart led me out to the center of the floor, weaving us around people I knew were staring at me. Why wouldn't they? They probably assumed I'd left. But I was tougher than that—at least Kozart was pushing me to feel like I was.

He slipped his hand free from mine. The lack of contact left me feeling bereft and vulnerable. But the feeling disappeared once he turned to face me, grasping my hips with his hands. Instinctively, I reached up and held onto his biceps. *Hello, biceps.* He moved us to the music. And he could dance. Not like a drunk guy who jumped into the middle of a dance floor at a club, but like a guy who knew how to use those hips.

As if he could read my mind, a cocky grin spread across his lips. The damn thing warmed my insides as he slipped his hands behind my back and pulled me closer to him. My back arched as I hit the wall of muscles beneath his hoodie. My hands drifted up to his shoulders, holding onto him as we moved. He had confidence that most guys my age didn't and it was sexy. His scent wrapped itself around me, a strange mixture of cologne and perfume. *Odd.*

I might've worried about how I looked grinding with a guy I just picked up in a bar, but the alcohol, mixed with my need to save face, urged me on. I closed my eyes and let Kozart guide my moves.

He buried his nose in my hair, moving his mouth toward my ear.

I pulled in a sharp breath.

"Is he still here?" he asked.

"He's the groom's brother, so probably."

"Your sister married his brother?"

"Yup, even more tragic, huh?"

The song ended and a slower one began. I took a step back, but Kozart pulled me closer, the small gesture meaning so much more than he—or even I—realized.

Since he was a good head taller than me, I rested my cheek against his shoulder.

"He's an idiot," Kozart said.

"Obviously."

He laughed and his breath tickled my bare shoulder. "What's your name?"

"Isn't it so much more interesting if you don't know?"

"Aubrey," my sister called from nearby.

So much for more interesting.

I lifted my head and twisted around to find my sister Caroline standing there in her gorgeous fitted white gown. She owned that room. And I didn't want her worrying about me on the biggest day of her life.

"What are you doing?" she asked, guilt plaguing her eyes.

"What's it look like I'm doing? I'm having an unforgettable time at my sister's wedding." I smiled way too wide for it to be authentic. And she knew it.

"Let's go talk," she said.

"I'm fine. Look. I'm dancing."

She looked to Kozart, her eyes narrowing suspiciously. She probably wondered where I found a guy on such short notice.

"I'm taking good care of her," he explained. "Just keep your bridesmaid and brother-in-law away."

"I told Jewel to leave," Caroline explained. Though for a newly married woman, she seemed to be having difficulty tearing her eyes away from Kozart.

"Go enjoy the rest of your night," I said. "I'm fine."

Her eyes finally jumped to mine, searching for the truth behind my lie.

"Go," I urged. "And get them to play some country music, would ya?"

Reluctantly, she turned and disappeared amongst the swaying bodies on the dance floor who all wanted to greet her.

"Country music?" Kozart asked, disgust dripping from his words.

"Is there any other genre?"

"Yup," he said flatly, pulling me back to him. "*Aubrey.*"

"You caught that, huh?"

"As if the name was shouted from the highest mountain and echoed throughout the room."

I laughed.

"It's fitting."

"What?"

"Your pretty name," he said.

"Watch out. I may mistake your kindness as you stalking my profile."

His entire body shook with silent laughter as he pressed his lips to the crown of my head. "It's nice to meet you, Aubrey."

The song ended and a popular dance song pumped through the speakers. "I need a drink. Do you need a drink?" I asked, suddenly feeling flustered. He'd called me pretty *twice* and kissed my head. What the hell was happening?

He flashed another cocky grin. "I could go for another," he said, amused by my flustered-ness.

Stupid mind reader.

I turned to walk away, but he grabbed my hand and pulled me back to walk alongside him, in no rush at all. He wanted everyone to look at us. And I liked that he was taking his fake-date duties seriously.

We stepped up to the bar and placed our order. Kozart turned and leaned against it, watching the people filling the room. "Show me."

"What?"

"Your ex."

I turned, my eyes scanning the room. I didn't have to search for long. Geoffrey's dark eyes were on mine. A cold shiver rushed up my spine. To think his gaze once elicited butterflies in my stomach. I'd been so foolish. So blind.

Kozart followed my gaze. "That him?"

"Hmm," I grunted.

Kozart stepped in front of me, blocking my view of my ex. He grabbed his ball cap and twisted it on his head so it was backward.

I stared into his icy blue eyes, the ones that were no longer concealed by the shade of his hat. His lips twitched in the corners, and I waited for whatever he planned to say. The seconds ticked by. My eyes never wavered from his. His hands finally lifted to my cheeks, cupping them gently. I pulled in a quick breath as he leaned down and captured my lips with his.

His tongue probed my lips, seeking access. I was in no condition—mentally or physically—to refuse. My lips parted and my tongue greeted his in an easy dance. I didn't care that my ex could see. I didn't care he was a stranger. I didn't care we were at my sister's wedding after I'd just been singled up. All I cared about was the way he was making me feel and the need for it to continue for as long as humanly possible. Kozart could kiss. That was for damn sure.

Much too soon, he pulled away, leaving me embarrassingly breathless.

My entire body hummed as I stared at him, surprised and turned on beyond reason. I'd just met the freaking guy and his kiss had turned my insides giddy and my knees to jelly.

"That'll show him," he said, dragging his thumb across his damp bottom lip before twisting his hat back around on his head.

I blinked, reality hitting me hard. That's why he'd kissed me. To help me get back at my ex. My emotions were so out of whack I'd actually believed the kiss was real. I was hopeless.

I turned to the bar and grabbed the glass, downing my entire drink. I just needed this night to end.

CHAPTER THREE

Kozart

"Easy does it," I said, gripping Aubrey's arm as we walked down the third-floor hallway.

Her steps were uneven and her giggle adorable. "You know when I said I wasn't drunk? Well, I'm totally drunk right now."

I chuckled as I slipped the key card from her hand. "Just a few more feet." I stopped us in front of room 304 and scanned the card. The door clicked and Aubrey pushed it open, practically falling inside. I reached out and caught her. She snort-laughed.

Drunk girls were normally a huge turn-off for me, but she was a pleasant surprise. It was probably because her drunkenness wasn't her trying to work up the nerve to approach me. She was drunk because she just didn't know what else to do to make it through the hellish night she'd had.

That's the reason I joined her at the wedding. I hated fucking weddings. But what I hated more were dickheads who thought they could have their cake and eat it too. I stayed single so I wouldn't be that guy. I knew I wanted to eat lots of cake. It wasn't fair to anyone, me included, to settle down.

"What the fuck?"

My head snapped to my left. Aubrey's ex lay on the king-sized hotel bed in nothing but his boxers.

"I swear to God," Aubrey said, her eyes shooting daggers at the dickhead in her bed. "If you're not out of here in two seconds, I will kill you with my bare hands."

"Who the hell is *he*?" her ex asked, his eyes narrowed on me.

"You lost the right to ask the second you fucked someone else," I answered for her.

His eyes shot to Aubrey. "Picking up guys at hotels, Aubs. That's a new low even for you."

She glared at him. "You think you can show up here and try to make me feel bad for what *I* do? You're such an asshole."

I crossed my arms and stared down at him still on her bed, my brow raised. "That sounded like the lady telling you to get the fuck out of her room."

"Wow, a classy one," he said to Aubrey.

"I wasn't the one fucking a bridesmaid when my girlfriend was in the same hotel," I countered.

He hopped off the bed, and for a second I thought he was coming for me. *That* would've been comical. But he grabbed his clothes from the nearby chair instead. *Pussy.*

"If you think she's gonna give it up," he said to me with a snare on his lips. "Don't get too excited. She's not that good."

My mouth opened, my clenching fists dropping to my sides.

He bent and grabbed his shoes from the floor. When he stood back up, I was in his space. "If she's too classy to hit you, I'd love a shot."

"Try it," he said, lifting his chin to show he had balls.

"He's not worth it," Aubrey said as she moved to the door and pulled it open. "Thanks for making this so easy on me, Geoffrey. I have no idea what I ever saw in you."

Though I really wanted one good shot at the douchebag, I just smirked at him. "You heard her. You're not worth it."

He growled low in his throat and turned, stopping in front of Aubrey. "Sleep with him and I'll never take you back."

She laughed in his face. "Promise?"

Aubrey

The banging in my head made it impossible to open my eyes. I pulled the blankets tighter around me, hoping my warm cocoon would help me fight off the killer hangover awaiting me.

The previous night had been a blur. One giant swirling tornado of a blur.

Wait.

My eyes snapped open. I winced as the bright sunlight filtering into the hotel room blinded me. Once I blinked away the fuzzy white cloud in my eyes, I braced myself for who I might find in my bed.

My eyes shifted slowly to the left.

One long breath of relief whooshed out of me as I stared at the empty spot beside me.

What happened after Kozart kissed me? Had he walked me back to my room? Left me in the lobby? How did I even get here?

"Morning," a deep voiced greeted me.

I sprang upright, gasping when I realized I wore only my strapless bra and panties. I tugged the sheets up, covering all but my head.

"Nothing I haven't seen already," Kozart said, standing in the doorway of the bathroom in his hat and jeans, his lips twitching wildly. His bare chest and tatted-up muscles were difficult to ignore. The guy was jacked and he clearly knew I'd have difficulty not drinking him in.

I tightened my grip on the sheets, like that would somehow protect me from him. From the embarrassment of my drunkenness. From hearing what happened between us last night. "Did you take my clothes off?"

He pointed to himself. "No. You had a grand ole time stripping down for me."

A cold fear rushed through me. "I did?"

"Oh, yeah. Better than a show in a Vegas strip club."

"You're lying."

A lopsided grin tipped his lips. "Yes. I'm lying. You got undressed while I was in there." He ticked his head behind him into the bathroom.

"Where did *you* sleep?"

"Listen, I can only be so much of a gentleman."

Confused, my brows inverted.

"I wasn't about to sleep in that hard-ass chair when there was a perfectly good spot beside you."

My gaze drifted to the sheets, my eyes avoiding his. "Did we…?"

"We did not. You were asleep when I got back out here."

My eyes lifted to his. "You could've gone back to your room."

He crossed his arms. "Yes. I could've gone back to my room, but I didn't feel right leaving you alone after your ex left."

I gasped. "He was here?"

He tilted his head. "You don't remember?"

I shook my head, racking my brain for the details.

"You kicked his ass out."

"I did?" Laughter burst out of me. "Even when I'm drunk I'm awesome."

He laughed, though his laughter faded into a long stretch of silence that passed between us.

"So…" I finally said. "You headed out now or are you in town longer?"

"Nope, heading home today."

"Where's home?"

He stared at me for a long time, as if he knew something I didn't. "Nashville."

"You don't have an accent," I said.

He chuckled as he moved to the desk chair where his hoodie lay draped over the back.

Turning his back to me, he pulled off his hat to reveal dirty blond hair—short on the sides and longer on top. I caught a glimpse of a colorful tattoo spanning the top of his back from shoulder blade to shoulder blade. An eagle maybe. But it was concealed as soon as he tugged his hoodie over his head. He turned to look at me, holding my University of Tennessee T-shirt he'd picked up from the dresser. "Did you go here?"

"I'm a senior. Speech pathology major."

"No kidding?"

I shook my head.

"I used to stutter when I was a kid," he admitted.

"I'm taking a stuttering class this semester. Did you see a speech pathologist?"

His eyes dodged mine as he shook his head, and I wondered why he hadn't.

"Well, it seems like yours disappeared."

"In high school."

"Does it ever happen now?"

He shrugged. "Only once in a great while when I'm extremely nervous."

I nodded, understanding that happened to adults who once stuttered during stressful situations. "So, where'd you go to college?" I asked.

"I didn't. But I've been on your campus a couple times."

"Oh, yeah?"

"Been to some football games."

"Maybe we'll run into each other sometime."

He shrugged. "I travel a lot, so..."

I inwardly cringed, knowing a brush-off when I heard one. "Well, thanks for helping last night."

"I'm not one to leave a damsel in distress."

"I'm not a damsel in distress."

He stared across the room at me. "Yeah. I'm starting to see that."

We both fell silent.

After a moment, he pushed off the dresser and walked to the side of the bed. I held my breath as he leaned down, dropping a kiss to the top of my head. "Take care of yourself, Aubrey."

"I'll be fine."

"I know you will." He turned and walked to the door.

I expected him to turn once he reached it, but he didn't. He pulled the door open and walked out, disappearing as if he'd never even been there.

I fell back onto the bed and exhaled.

Waking up to Kozart in my room stopped me from waking up and dwelling on how my life was turned upside-down yesterday. I couldn't roll into a ball and pity myself for losing everything in the blink of an eye. But now that I lay in silence...alone...it's all I could think about.

What was I supposed to do now?

School began in a few days, and I was supposed to be moving in with Geoffrey. That had always been the plan for our senior year. Live together and plan our future. Now what?

Could I crash with my friends—who'd already rented out their fourth room—until I found a place to live?

I closed my eyes and willed away any tears that threatened to fall.

Geoffrey and I had so many plans. What did I do now that he'd destroyed them?

There was a knock on my door.

I jolted up.

Please don't be Geoffrey.

I slipped out of bed, grabbing the Tennessee T-shirt from the dresser and pulling it over my head. I moved to the door and peeked through the peep hole. I dragged in a deep breath, definitely unprepared for this conversation, but pulled the door open nonetheless. "Hey."

"Hi," my sister said as she peeked over my shoulder, clearly checking to see if I had any guests.

"He just left," I informed her.

"Oh my God," she gushed, rushing into my room. "I can't believe he stayed in here."

"Don't get too excited. I passed out." I closed the door and turned to her. "At least that's what Kozart told me."

"You call him Kozart?" she giggled.

My brows pinched. "That's his name."

A look of realization swept over her features. "You don't know who he is."

"I met him in the bar. It wasn't like I had a guy on standby for when my boyfriend cheated on me."

Her nose wrinkled. "I'm confused."

"Why?"

"You just spent the night with Z Savage," she squealed as she dropped down onto the bed.

"Z Savage?"

"From Savage Beasts."

"What's Savage Beasts?"

She smacked her palm against her forehead. "The band."

"He's in a band?"

"He *is* the band. How do you not know that?"

"I listen to country."

"But he's like the hottest rock star on the planet."

"I don't like rock."

She shook her head at my obvious oblivion. "He's so damn hot. It took everything in me not to get a picture with him last night."

"Well, my night with a rock star was probably one for the record books. No sex, drugs, or rock and roll. Just me asleep."

"You better lie and tell everyone you slept with him, because technically you slept in the same bed, right?"

I nodded, though I remembered nothing.

She grabbed the pillow from where he slept and sniffed it. "He smells so good."

"You're sick."

"I can't believe you're not more excited."

"Why would I be excited? I've never heard of him *and* he's gone now."

"You didn't exchange numbers?"

I scoffed. "Why? To meet up again in the future to pass out on him?"

"You're gorgeous and newly single—Wait. You're not getting back with Geoffrey, are you?"

"Not a chance in hell."

Regret replaced the excitement in her eyes. "I'm so sorry."

"You didn't make him cheat on me with your friend."

"She's no friend of mine," she assured me. "We're done."

She didn't even need to say it. I knew she'd have my back.

"So, what now?" she asked.

I shrugged. "Go to school and avoid Geoffrey at all costs."

"I can't stand him."

"You shouldn't talk about your brother-in-law that way."

"He hurt my sister."

"Yeah, well. I think I was meant to learn the hard way about him. That way I'd stay far away."

"Doesn't make it hurt less."

"Well, Kozart, Z, whatever his name is, made me forget for a little bit."

"Imagine if you'd slept with him!"

I rolled my eyes. "I just meant, maybe I'll have an easier time getting over Geoffrey than I would've thought."

"You deserve someone amazing, Aubrey. There's not a doubt in my mind that you'll find him."

She was my sister, so she had to say that. But I would've given anything to believe it.

CHAPTER FOUR

Aubrey

What's almost as bad as being cheated on by your boyfriend at your sister's wedding? Attending the morning-after brunch alone when said cheater sat across the room laughing and carrying on with his family.

I sat with my parents, in my corner seat, my phone in my hand, searching for a place to live. In a few days, I'd be back at school and homeless.

Damn Geoffrey.

Damn me for being so dense.

Damn me for not realizing he was such an asshole.

I didn't deserve to be cheated on. I'd been a good girlfriend. Sure, I enjoyed partying with my friends on the weekends, but I never cheated. Never let myself be tempted beyond the point of no return.

Speaking of temptation.

My thoughts drifted to Kozart. My *kiss* with Kozart. My knee-quaking, moment-freezing kiss with a rock star. *That* was a temptation all in itself. But I was single now. I could kiss whoever I wanted. And last night, I really wanted to kiss Kozart.

I deserved knee-quaking kisses. I deserved a guy who'd walk in a room full of strangers with me to save the day. I knew, now more than ever, that what I'd had with Geoffrey never sizzled like that one kiss with Kozart.

I deserved amazing.

I deserved *someone* amazing.

My fingers drifted over the apps on my phone, curiosity getting the best of me. I typed *Z* into the search bar. My screen exploded with photos and articles about Savage Beasts and Z Savage. My eyes widened at the sweaty photos of Kozart on stage—shirtless and ripped—the microphone clutched in his fist and pressed to his lips as he belted out a song. I wondered what his voice sounded like when it filled an arena.

I scrolled through the photos—many were selfies with fans in the crowd or backstage at meet-and-greets. Others were of him sans ball cap, his dirty blond hair styled on red carpets at awards shows and other high-profile events. There was a never-ending parade of blondes, brunettes, and pink-haired girls in the pictures by his side. Oddly, no photos captured his smile. A smug smirk shone in all of them, like he knew something no one else did.

I wondered what it was.

Though none of the pictures caught him smiling, they definitely captured his blue eyes which dazzled the camera lens in each and every one.

My phone vibrated in my hand. A text appeared on the screen.

My stomach roiled at Geoffrey's words. **We need to talk.**

My thumbs bounced off the screen at a rapid pace. **Too late for that. Lose my number.** I glanced up at him across the room and watched as he read my response.

His eyes shot up.

I lifted my middle finger and scratched my cheek, and just like that, I was done with that chapter of my life. I didn't need him. I'd be perfectly fine spending my senior year of college wild and free. That's what life was about, wasn't it?

Living.

CHAPTER FIVE

Aubrey

"We're gonna have so much fun," Eliza said as I moved my final box into her condo on the outskirts of campus.

"We sure are," I said, though I wasn't as convinced as she was.

Eliza and I had been assigned as roommates freshmen year, but I'd lived with three of my other friends—blond triplets—sophomore and junior year who I had more in common with. Unfortunately, they'd rented their fourth room out when they thought I'd be living with Geoffrey. Eliza planned to live alone after her roommate decided not to return to Tennessee, but offered me the room once she heard about my situation. I was fortunate to call her a friend, even if we didn't share the same taste in movies, music, and…just about everything.

"Is it okay to be honest with you?" Eliza asked as she trudged up the stairs behind me in her black combat boots.

"You better," I said, entering the condo and walking down the hallway to my bedroom.

"I always thought Geoffrey was such a tool."

Laughter rushed out of me as I placed the box down on the floor by the window. "I wish I'd realized it sooner."

"You were in love," she said.

"It wasn't love. Love doesn't hurt. I can see that now."

"So, I don't have to worry about him coming in with that obnoxious cologne? That stuff made me sneeze. I think I was allergic to him."

We broke into laughter. And just like that, I knew I was home for the year.

* * *

The first week of school flew by, and the fact that I'd been able to avoid Geoffrey made it even better.

I was looking forward to a night out with my friends. They were in the living room blaring music and drinking while I finished getting ready. Eliza lay on my bed scrolling through the newsfeed on her phone.

"You sure you don't want to come with us?" I asked, looking at her through my mirror.

"Nope. Not my scene."

"It's a bar."

"Still. Not my scene."

I brushed on a tiny bit of mascara and I was ready to go. I turned to look at her. "Last chance."

Her eyes moved over my skinny jeans and low-plunging black top. "Should I turn my music up loud tonight?"

My nose scrunched. "What?"

She tipped her chin toward me. "With you looking that hot, I'm guessing you're not coming home alone."

I laughed. "I'm single and ready to have fun with my friends. I don't need a guy."

I left Eliza in my room and headed toward the living room to join my friends, known on campus as the triplets. It was unfortunate that people lumped them together as one entity. Just because they looked identical, didn't mean they were the same. If people took the time to get to know them, they'd learn that Marla was the responsible planner. Mandy was the party-girl but also super smart. And Melinda was the humanitarian, saving animals and homeless people in a single bound at a nearby shelter.

I stepped into the living room. The girls all wore jeans and some type of funky top and smiled when they spotted me—ready for my first night out as a single girl.

Mandy handed me a drink. "Here. You need this."

I took a sip and it burned going down. I shook off the unwelcome surprise as the warmth of it spread through my veins.

It took no time for us to make it to the bar. The bouncer, a guy we'd known since freshman year, motioned for us to cut the long line and let us through the doors. Mandy laid a nice big kiss on his lips, ensuring we'd be cutting the line all year.

Inside the bar-turned-club-at-night, the music blared. The bass shook the building. The floor vibrated beneath my feet as I followed my friends through the wave of people to the bar.

Marla ordered us a round of shots, and while we waited, my eyes scanned the packed room. It took no more than a few seconds to spot Geoffrey. His dark eyes widened when they locked on mine, and a sinking feeling filled my stomach.

"Here," Marla said, shouting over the music and pushing a shot my way.

I grabbed it, suddenly needing liquid courage more than I realized. I turned to my friends, we clinked our glasses together, then downed our shots. I was looking to have a good time and nothing was going to ruin that.

"Hi," Geoffrey's familiar voice breathed into my ear from behind.

I stilled.

"Aubrey," he continued.

Pulling in a breath, I turned slowly.

"Didn't you hear me?" he asked, his eyes staring into mine.

"Yup."

Melinda handed me a drink, and I downed it as Geoffrey looked on.

"Let's go!" Mandy called as she grabbed my hand and pulled me away from Geoffrey and onto the dance floor with Marla and Melinda following behind us.

Our bodies moved around the crowded space as if no one else was on the dance floor but us. I missed laughing and hanging out with my friends—without having to report back to anyone. I hadn't realized I'd done that. Even while I was out with my friends, I still always worried about Geoffrey. Now I only needed to worry about me.

The song ended and another began. The girls screamed. I wasn't much of a screamer, nor did I listen to the music they did, so I didn't know the song they were excited about.

Wait.

The hair on my arms stood on end as an electrical charge coasted over my body. That voice. That deep gravelly voice reverberating through the room. I looked up at the speakers, as if that would somehow reveal the singer. "Who sings this?" I asked, already fairly certain I knew the answer.

"Zzzzzzzzzzzz!" Marla squealed.

I hadn't told my friends about my night with a rock star. I know it would've been on the forefront on most girls' minds, but I'd been humiliated. Lied to. And then I needed to find a place to stay. My tale of passing out on a rock star—who I didn't even know was a rock star—hadn't really been a priority.

Kozart's voice pounded through me as he sang about pain and moving on. I wished I knew the words so I could sing along with the rest of the bar. But this country girl didn't.

Strong hands grasped my hips from behind. I stilled. Someone leaned in and brushed my ear with his lips as he spoke. "I've missed you."

I spun around.

Geoffrey gazed down at me. "*So* much."

My hands shot to his chest, and I pressed him away, stopping him from leaning down and kissing me. "Woah. Not happening."

Mandy pushed in between us, slamming her hands into Geoffrey's chest. "If you don't get the hell away from her, I will have you escorted out of here."

He glared at her, his annoyance playing out across his face. His eyes cut back to mine. "I'm serious, Aubs. This can't be over." He backed away, turning and disappearing into the crowd.

Seriously?

I turned back to my friends who shook their heads in disgust. And while I felt just as disgusted as them, I wasn't going to allow Geoffrey to ruin another night.

* * *

I climbed into bed feeling exhausted and drunk. I'd needed the night out. Needed to remember what it felt like to be a college girl with no restrictions. Melinda saw Geoffrey leave shorty after I rejected him and Mandy threatened him, which made for a much better night.

I was just about to doze off when my phone vibrated beside me on my nightstand. I expected to find a photo from one of the triplets doing something crazy. We'd been known to send a drunk photo or ten after a late night out. But it wasn't them. It was a call from a number I didn't recognize. *Please don't be Geoffrey.*

I accepted the call and lifted my phone to my ear. "Hello?"

"Hi," a deep voice said.

"Who is this?"

"I got your info from a dating site."

My eyes widened. Oh. My. God. I harnessed the nervous excitement rippling in my belly. "You did, huh? I don't remember putting my phone number down when I filled out my profile."

"Weird," he mused.

"Very."

A long silence passed. I listened to his breathing. Listened for sounds that would indicate he'd just come offstage, but there was only silence.

"So, let me ask you," I said, hating silence almost as much as Geoffrey. "What drew you to my profile? Was it the passed-out-on-the-bar part?"

He chuckled, and the low sound nestled deep inside of me. "Maybe."

"How about the amazing dancer part? I thought that highlighted my diversity."

He chuckled again, and I was beginning to enjoy the sound more than I should. "Could've been that part."

Another silence passed. This time I waited him out. He called *me* after all.

"How are you?" he finally asked.

"Better than last time you saw me. Actually, I *am* drunk, but that's just because I went out tonight to let loose with my friends now that I'm back at school."

"Run into the dick?"

"Unfortunately."

"That sucks."

Another long silence. Come on, Kozart. Why'd you call?

"I was thinking about you," he said, as if he'd heard my internal question.

Was he a mind reader? "Oh yeah?"

"Yeah."

"So, you stalked my profile?"

"Nah. I called myself from your phone when you were asleep so I'd have your number."

"Why'd you want my number? I know it wasn't my stellar skills in the sack."

"Don't underestimate the power of the drunken snore."

I laughed. "I don't snore."

"Oh, but you do."

"And yet, here you are."

He chuckled again and I wondered if it was his way of not having to respond.

A siren bellowed somewhere in the background through the phone as I waited him out.

"Send me your picture," he said.

"What?"

"I don't have a picture of you."

"Why would you?"

"Well, we did sleep together."

"So, you keep pictures of all the girls you sleep with?"

"Humor me," he said.

"How do I know you're not some perv who plans to do weird things with it?"

"If I *am* some perv, you let me sleep in bed with you."

"I was unconscious."

"Yes, and I didn't take advantage of you."

"That I know of," I countered.

"Do you have an answer for everything?"

"Yup."

"So, no picture?"

"Nope."

"Fair enough. It was kind of a pervy thing to ask."

"You should add that to *your* dating profile."

He laughed, and the sound sent crazy vibrations through my nerve endings. "I'm glad I called."

"I'm glad I could amuse you at two in the morning."

Silence.

Damn him.

"Goodnight, Aubrey," he drawled.

"Goodnight, Kozart." I ended the call, wondering why he'd called me. Why he'd called himself from my phone in the first place. Why a rock star wanted a photo of me when I saw the girls he usually hung with.

Those were the thoughts swirling through my drunken mind before sleep pulled me under.

CHAPTER SIX

Aubrey

My phone buzzed in my messenger bag during a two-hour lecture in philosophy. I glanced at the students around me. They didn't bother to even look my way. Most of them had dozed off or typed what the professor assumed were notes on their laptops, while they were actually playing games or checking their social media newsfeeds.

I slipped my phone out of my bag to find a text from Kozart on my screen. **Do you know who I am?**

My thumbs pounded away. **My stalker?**

Good answer.

I'm in class right now, so I hope you're not looking for a picture.

You know me so well.

That couldn't have been further from the truth. I didn't know him at all. And even after the phone call the other night, I hadn't looked him up. Something inside me told me I didn't want to know anything he didn't tell me. Nor did I want to slip and reveal something I knew from stalking him. So, I promised myself I'd wait him out. If he called again, maybe I'd learn more from him. And if he didn't, maybe I'd stalk his ass.

Learning anything exciting?

Nope. What are you up to?

Just driving.

You shouldn't text and drive.

I'm not driving. I'm on a bus.

Where you headed?
Tampa.
Beach?
Nah. Got work to do.
Work, huh? Wasn't touching that one. **Well, good
luck with that.**
Enjoy your class, Aubrey.
Enjoy your work, stalker ;-)

I stuffed my phone in my bag and drew a deep breath.
What do you want from me, Kozart Savage? What do
you want?

* * *

I lay on my bed with my laptop in front of me, typing
out a paper. Music played from my phone. When that
playlist ended, I reached for my phone to play a different
one.

I chewed on my bottom lip in deliberation. Then I
gave in, typing in 'Savage Beasts.' A long playlist
appeared. I clicked on shuffle and let the music play.

The first song began with a long guitar solo before
Kozart's voice filtered through the speaker, slow and
eerie. His words were ominous, his pain evident. The
drums came through in the chorus and his voice grew
louder and more tortured. I was a country music girl
through and through, but this song and Kozart's pain-
stricken words made me long to help him. To heal him.

God, I was losing it.

I couldn't concentrate on my paper. I rolled onto my
back and closed my eyes, listening to the entire playlist.
By the end, I wasn't necessarily a fan, but I was intrigued.
Had Kozart written the songs? Were those *his* thoughts
and feelings? I definitely enjoyed the ballads more than
the heavier rock songs. I think that was partially due to
the fact that I wasn't a fan of hearing anger in Kozart's

voice. It was such a stark contrast to the guy who'd come to my rescue. But I could see why rock fans enjoyed it. It definitely gave them something to rage out to.

CHAPTER SEVEN

Kozart

I walked offstage, grabbing a bottle of water from the top of the speaker and chugging it. Once backstage, I was joined by my bandmates surrounded by some girls our tour manager brought back to greet us once we came offstage.

We had another show in Tampa the following night, so the guys weren't in a rush to get back to the hotel, dropping down on the leather sofas and lounging with the groupies. I, however, was psyched to get back to the hotel so I could get some sleep. I was someone who didn't sleep. If I got more than two uninterrupted hours per night it was a miracle. But, since Tennessee, I'd been sleeping.

"I'll catch you guys on the bus," I said, twisting off the cap of my water and chugging the rest of it.

"Stay and have a drink," Treyton called.

"Not tonight," I said, heading to the back exit of the arena and right onto the bus. I stripped down and hopped into the shower, mentally reviewing my performance as the water cascaded over my body. There were things I wanted to switch up the next night in case some of the same fans attended both shows. And I was considering adding a new cover song with no instruments, just me on stage with a guitar and a spotlight.

Ten minutes later, I felt the bus move. I knew we were on our way back to the hotel, so I stepped out of the shower and wrapped a towel around my waist before heading to my room in the back of the bus to get dressed.

"Hey, bro," Treyton said.

My head shot to my right. Treyton and the other guys were surrounded by the fucking groupies from the arena up front in our bus' sitting area. The groupies' eyes drank in my half-naked tatted-up body. One licked her cherry red lips, and the other pulled out her phone. Reggie, our new bodyguard who was nearby, ripped it from her hand.

On a normal night, I could've beckoned Miss Cherry Red with the crook of my finger and fucked her in my bed. Tonight, I wasn't feeling it. I actually hadn't indulged since the two blondes in Tennessee. Maybe it had gotten old. Hell, maybe *I* was getting old. Old at twenty-five. Go figure.

Without a word, I turned and headed to my room, sliding the door closed to keep the rest of the world out. I actually hated being surrounded by people. *Ironic, I know.* I just hated the constant pressure of being "on" even when I was in a private space. I missed my anonymity. Missed knowing why people wanted to be around me. Missed being treated like I wasn't perfect, because I *wasn't* fucking perfect. That's for damn sure.

The bus lurched to a stop a few minutes later. *Thank fuck.*

I threw a T-shirt over my head, slipped into basketball shorts, and pulled my ball cap low on my head. When I heard everyone else get off the bus, I slid open my bedroom door. The bus sat idling behind the hotel, and our bodyguard stood at the staff entrance, waiting for me. He knew how I felt about being seen with groupies—even when *I* was the one bringing them back with us.

"Thanks, man," I said to Reggie as I stepped off the bus and walked inside.

He nodded, never saying much of anything. I think it's why our tour manager hired him. He knew I was sick of ass-kissers and people wanting to be up in my business.

Avoiding the lobby, I followed Reggie up the stairs to the third floor, where we got on the elevator that took us to the top floor. As we stepped out of the elevator and made our way down the hallway toward the penthouse, he handed me a key card and ticked his head to the left.

"Seriously?"

He nodded.

"Thank you," I said as I took the card and scanned it on the door—a door that didn't belong to the penthouse. I pushed open the door to find a king-sized bed and a normal sized room.

Perfect.

I left Reggie in the hallway and made my way over to the bed, dropping down onto my back and enjoying the silence. I lay there for a long time, so grateful for the time alone. It's crazy how alone one can feel in a room full of people. Especially, when those people thought they knew me, but had no fucking clue who I was or what I'd been through.

I knew I was on the verge of sleep, so I reached down and grabbed my phone from my pocket, checking the screen. A few missed calls from my publicist. Nothing important as usual.

I wondered why Aubrey hadn't called me. She clearly had my number now. Most girls would've texted immediately, usually sending naked pictures of some sort—thinking that's what every rock star liked. Don't get me wrong. I was not opposed to naked pictures. I welcomed them. But that wasn't the only thing I was about.

I thought back to Aubrey—just awoken from the sunlight in the hotel room, her hair messy and cheeks flushed. An unfamiliar anxiousness formed in my gut. Why *hadn't* she called me? Not having a girl throw herself at me was new for me. I wondered if it's what would've happened if I wasn't famous. Would girls not have been interested in me? Aubrey didn't know who I was and didn't call. Maybe girls only wanted me when they knew who I was. Maybe that's all I had going for me. Maybe the real me wasn't enough.

I needed to know what it was with Aubrey.

I touched my camera icon on my phone, reversing the screen so I could see myself, head on the pillow with my ball cap low on my head. I thought back to her in the bar giving me sass and I couldn't help but smile. Rock stars didn't smile. At least that's what I told myself since I had difficulty smiling and actually meaning it. But I snapped the picture anyway and sent it off with a text.

Aubrey

My phone vibrated as I finished up my essay. I grabbed it. Kozart's picture filled the screen with a message beneath it. **Now show me yours.**

I laughed as I checked the time. Just after midnight. Had he called me right after his show? Were there no groupies for him tonight or was he just quick with his post-concert activities?

Since I wasn't supposed to know who he was, I couldn't ask. So, I just responded the only way I could. **I believe the saying is, I'll show you mine if you show me yours. I'm feeling let down I only got a face shot.** I laughed to myself as I watched the three dots bouncing.

His text appeared quickly. **Be careful what you wish for.**

I swallowed down my sudden nerves. I hadn't really thought through what he could send back. My thumbs bounced off the screen. **Jk. No dick pics please.**

I'm still waiting on you…

I thought for a minute. **I think you want my picture bc you were drunk the night we met and can't remember what I look like.**

Wrong.

Even his texts were confident, I thought, as I challenged him with my own. **Prove it.**

I was with you in the morning.

Dammit.

I contemplated my next move. What was the worst that could happen from sending an innocent picture? I climbed off my bed and checked myself in the mirror. I fixed my waves into place and pinched my cheeks to give them a touch of color.

Here goes nothing.

I clicked on the camera and reversed the screen so I could see myself. I smiled and snapped a photo. I checked it. *Ugh.* I tried again, this time not trying to smile so wide. I snapped the photo and checked it. A little better. I couldn't spend the entire night doing a photo shoot, so I sent it off to him. **Happy?**

There was a long pause as I lay back on my bed.

No dots appeared.

What the hell?

Was he disappointed I'd given in? Disappointed by how I looked?

The dots eventually started bouncing. **Immensely.**

What are you gonna do with it?

His text came quickly. **Something pervy.**

I snorted as I replied. **Next time I see you, my picture better be your screensaver.**

Will there be a next time?

Stalkers always meet up with their prey. I responded, laughing aloud at my witty response.

Lol!

* * *

I piled toppings high on my frozen yogurt in the fro-yo shop in the student union, so excited to get home to eat it.

"Hey, Aubs," Geoffrey said from behind me.

And, my appetite was lost.

I continued pouring multi-color sprinkles on my yogurt, hoping my silence caused him to go away.

"Aubrey," he persisted.

I begrudgingly turned to face him. "What?"

"Don't be like that," Geoffrey said, his hands gripping the straps of his backpack.

"Like what?"

"Like the way you're being."

I cocked my head. "What do you want from me?"

"I want us to be good."

A humorless laugh escaped me. "Good?"

He nodded.

"Why?"

"Because this wasn't supposed to be like this."

"You're right. You weren't supposed to cheat on me."

His head dropped back and he huffed his exasperation.

I turned back to my frozen yogurt and grabbed a lid, smooshing it down on top of the mess I'd created.

His chest pressed into my back. I froze, almost scared to have him touching me. His familiar scent of cologne blasted its way into my senses. Eliza was right about it. I nearly gagged on it now. "We were good together," he breathed into my ear.

"I know. Then you screwed it up," I said, slipping away from him and hurrying to the cash register.

He didn't follow. And I didn't look back.

CHAPTER EIGHT

Aubrey

"Shots!" Mandy shrieked as she passed them down the bar to the girls and me.

I threw back my shot and felt the liquor spread through me, much like the previous three. I was becoming a total lush these days, but I was twenty-one and I wasn't driving home. I knew how to stay safe. I never left the bar alone. I never accepted a drink from someone I didn't know. And I never left my drinks unattended.

"Let's dance," Melinda called to us and we followed her onto the dance floor.

Our bodies moved to the hip-hop song blaring through the speakers, our hearts thumping with every beat of the song. The flashing lights made it difficult to see outside our circle which probably added to our we-don't-give-a-damn attitudes as we tore up the dance floor.

The song ended and a slow one began. Ugh. "I've gotta pee," I called to my friends who nodded their understanding as they searched for dance partners.

I spun on my wedges and wove my way through the bodies swaying to the music. I reached the long line outside the girls' restroom and took my spot in the back. I slipped my phone from my back pocket and checked it. No calls. No messages.

Kozart hadn't reached out since the night I sent him my picture. I wondered if he *had* forgotten what I looked like and now regretted calling me.

What did I expect? He was a rock star with girls at every stop. I was just one of many he'd met. Though, I was probably the only one he *hadn't* actually slept with.

I eventually reached the front of the line and squeezed into the tiny bathroom stall, doing my business, then washing my hands and checking myself in the small mirror. My makeup had stayed in place, unusual after a night of dancing. I twisted a few waves around my finger to tame them back into place.

The music in the bar had changed to a party anthem. I gave myself one last look and grabbed the handle on the door. I stepped out, gasping as someone grabbed my arm and pulled me out the nearby exit door.

My heart raced as I pulled free, spinning around in the dark alley we'd ended up in.

Kozart stood in front of me, a ball cap pulled down low on his head and a smirk on his face.

My eyes widened. "What are you doing here?"

He dug his hands into the pockets of his torn jeans. "I was in the neighborhood."

I glanced around the windowless alley with its giant dumpsters and foul odor.

"I was in *town*," he clarified. "I just wanted to grab a drink and low and behold, here you are."

"Said every good stalker."

He threw his head back and laughed. The sound was just as sexy as it was over the phone, if not more as it echoed in the alley.

"And I'm sure I don't need to mention the dragging-me-out-of-the-bar-into-a-dark-alley thing," I added.

He chuckled, his eyes lowering to the pavement.

I motioned toward the closed door where muffled music tried to escape. "You could've just come up to me in there."

He shrugged, and we both knew why he couldn't hang out in a crowded bar. But would he finally say it? "You wanna go somewhere quiet and grab a drink?" he asked.

"So, not back inside?"

He shook his head.

"I don't have a car."

He shrugged. "We can walk."

I contemplated the crazy situation for a moment. I would be breaking most of my rules by leaving with him. But I trusted the guy I met in the hotel bar. The one who saved me from complete humiliation. The one who danced with me and kissed me to help me save face. The one who slept in my bed and didn't touch me. The one who called because he claimed to be thinking about me.

I slipped out my phone. "I need to let my friends know I'm leaving with my stalker. Should I forward them your picture in case I go missing?"

"I'd rather you not."

Again, we both knew why.

I wondered which of us would break first. "Fine. But I better not disappear."

He chuckled as I sent off the text.

"So, where to?"

"You tell me. This is your town."

"Where are you staying?" I asked.

"Not too far from here. The Mapleleaf."

"Let's go there."

He lifted a brow.

"Not to your *room*. To the bar."

He motioned toward the road with his signature smirk. "Let's go."

We walked along the quiet street, our arms brushing from time to time. The occasional car passed by, interrupting my thoughts and our uncomfortable silence. What in the world was he doing here? Did we really just run into each other randomly? Seemed a little too coincidental to me. And if he *had* sought me out, why wasn't he talking?

"So…" I finally said.

"So," he said.

"You gonna tell me why you're in town?"

"Work."

"What kind of work?"

His eyes searched the sidewalk for an answer that wasn't beneath his feet. "Would it be weird if I didn't say?"

"Extremely. And, I've gotta tell ya, my imagination is running wild right now with possibilities."

"Like?"

Shit. "Male escort?"

He burst into laughter. "No."

"You'd probably make some good money."

"Yeah?"

I cocked my head. "Come on. You know you're hot."

He averted my gaze. "What else?"

"Hockey player?"

"I've got all my teeth."

"Good point…how about…" I couldn't bring myself to say rock star, though every fiber of my being told me to come clean. "Assassin?"

"Assassin?"

"Yeah. You seem to travel a lot. Don't assassins travel when they're hunting someone down?"

He shrugged. "If that were the case, you'd be my hit."

"Another good point. You don't plan to kill me, do you?"

He chuckled as we neared the Mapleleaf Hotel—one of the oldest and most prestigious in the city. Suddenly, his laughter dissipated. A small group of girls had gathered by the main entrance of the hotel.

Kozart stopped, his eyes jumping from the front of the hotel to the back. He looked to me with desperation in his eyes. "I know this isn't going to prove I'm really not a stalker—or assassin for that matter, but is there any way you'd be willing to trust me enough to go around back to the staff entrance?"

"You know you're going to have to come clean sooner or later."

"I was hoping later."

I gave a quick glance to the girls out front. They'd be so envious if they saw me with Kozart. "Okay. But only if you promise."

He nodded, before pulling out his phone and sending a quick text to someone. He slipped it back in his pocket and grabbed hold of my hand. An unfamiliar numbness spread through my hand as he whisked me toward the back entrance, out of sight of the fans who stood in front hoping to catch a glimpse of him.

We reached the door in the rear of the hotel. Kozart pounded twice on it with the side of his fist. A big man with a nondescript black T-shirt pushed open the door and let us in without a word. Kozart mumbled, "Thanks," as he moved us past him and through the hotel kitchen.

The few kitchen workers who appeared to be cleaning up for the night didn't even bother looking at us.

Kozart peeked through the door window. When he sensed the coast was clear, he moved us through the lobby and into a small restaurant. It was quiet and empty, probably because it had already closed for the night. "Mind if we go in here and not the bar?"

"It looks closed."

"It's fine." He led me to the back corner of the restaurant where no one would see us.

I slipped into a chair as he sat across from me. He pulled out his phone and placed a quick call. "Hey, I'm in the restaurant. Can you have them bring out some appetizers and—" He looked to me. "What would you like to drink?"

"Whatever you're having."

"Two beers," he said into the phone before hanging up and laying his phone on the table.

"Does everyone do what you ask?"

He smirked. "*You're* here with me, aren't you?"

I stifled a grin. "You asked nicely." I glanced to his phone. "Let me see your screensaver."

"No."

"Why not?"

"Because I don't want you to be mad."

"Why would I be mad?"

Reluctantly, he lifted it. The generic screensaver that came with the phone filled the screen.

My eyes widened facetiously. "You *are* saving it for pervy things."

He tossed his head back and laughed. "You got me."

A waiter interrupted, delivering two beers. He offered up two glasses and we both waved him off.

I lifted my bottle to my lips and took a long drink. Kozart did the same, and I wondered if I made him as nervous as he was making me.

"I hope I didn't ruin your night," he said, his blue eyes gazing at me.

"You didn't really leave me much choice. I felt sorry for you."

He chuckled.

I took another drink of my beer, needing liquid courage to be with him knowing what I knew. "So…"

"So," he said.

"You promised to come clean."

He tilted his head, his gaze moving over my face. "I did?"

"You did."

His teeth dragged over his bottom lip, seemingly stalling—or thinking of something clever to say.

Though the wait was killing me, I waited him out.

His eyes drifted to everything but me.

Grrrr. "Tell me something about yourself, Kozart."

He tipped his head to the side. "Tell you what?"

"I don't know. How about…something no one else knows."

A flicker of amusement lit his eyes. "Why?"

"Because that's what people talk about when they meet the person they've been matched up with on a dating site."

He chuckled again. "Something no one knows, huh?"

I nodded.

His eyes lifted to the dim light above our table as he contemplated his response. "I like long walks on the beach at sunset."

Laughter burst out of me.

"And candlelit bubble baths."

I cocked my head.

"Oh, and don't forget poetry."

"You're one deep dude, you know that?"

He smiled.

The waiter interrupted again, this time delivering two trays of assorted appetizers, enough for ten people.

I lifted a brow at Kozart. "A deep dude *with* a big appetite."

"My profile's growing by the minute."

I smiled, knowing he didn't need a dating profile. He could have any girl he wanted.

He reached for a chicken skewer. "Dig in."

I grabbed a battered shrimp and gnawed into it, savoring the taste.

"Hungry?"

"Very," I said with my mouth full.

"I'm glad I found you," he said before lifting his bottle to his mouth.

"Was I lost?"

He shook his head. "I think I was."

"You're not anymore?"

He shrugged. "It doesn't feel that way right now."

I tried to quell the butterflies taking flight in my belly by lifting my bottle to my lips and swigging my beer. But good Lord. *He was good.* "How long are you in town?"

"Depends."

"On what?"

"If you'll agree to spend the night with me."

My entire face went slack, suddenly feeling like he was propositioning me.

"That sounded better in my head," he admitted.

"I don't know what it was about my profile that gave you the idea that I was *that* type of girl, but you're wrong."

He chuckled. "Is that a no?"

"It's a…what's in it for me?"

"You get to spend the night with me. Then I've got something to show you tomorrow—if you're interested."

"Should I be scared?"

"Very."

I stifled a smile and considered what he'd asked. "I don't have any clothes with me."

"I've got a T-shirt you can wear."

"I'm not having sex with you."

"Never asked you to."

A pit formed in my stomach as we picked at the food in silence. Was he really not interested in me that way?

"That's not saying I wouldn't be open to it if you were," he added with a grin.

I swigged the rest of my beer and lowered the empty bottle to the table a little louder than I'd meant to. "Fine."

"Fine?"

"Yup. But if you try anything pervy, I *will* Taser you."

"Taser me?"

I nodded.

He bent his head to look at my skinny jeans under the table. There was clearly nowhere to hold a Taser. We both knew it. He smirked before drinking the rest of his beer and glancing at the hardly touched food. "You want anything else or should I have them bring the rest up to my room."

I shook my head. "I'm good."

He threw some cash down on the table and stood. He again took my hand, helping me out of my chair and leading me to the stairwell.

"Stairwells are notorious for attacks on women," I said.

"Well, then you're lucky you've got your Taser."

I laughed as we climbed the first flight of stairs. "Glad I wore wedges."

He glanced down at my feet. "Shit, I wasn't thinking."

"No problem." I slipped them off and carried them.

He opened the door to the second floor and walked us down the hallway to the bank of elevators.

"I was fine," I assured him.

"I know. I do this out of habit."

Once the elevator arrived, we stepped inside. The doors closed and he pressed the button for the twenty-fifth floor. We were suddenly very alone. Soft music played as the elevator climbed to the top. Neither of us looked at each other or said a word.

Too many thoughts whirled through my head. Why in the world had I agreed to stay the night with him? Was it the recollection of our kiss? Or was it the excitement I felt every time he called me?

The bell chimed as the elevator stopped and the doors split apart. I followed Kozart out and down the quiet hallway. Were we going to the penthouse? Were his bandmates already there? Would there be groupies? I suddenly felt uneasy. Was *I* a groupie?

Kozart stopped halfway down the hallway and turned to a door on our left. He scanned his keycard and the door unlocked.

My lungs expanded on a long, deep breath as he pushed open the door and flipped on the light. I stepped inside first. A king-sized bed was the focal point in the center of the normal-sized hotel room. There were no liquor bottles, drugs, or panties strewn around the room. There was a suitcase on the luggage rack, but besides that, the room appeared unoccupied.

"One bed?" I asked with a lifted brow.

"Didn't know I'd have company."

"Is that so?"

A knowing grin slipped across his face.

"That's right," I said as I slowly circled the small room. "You just *happened* to run into me."

"Crazy how that happened."

I met his gaze.

Given the honesty I was seeking, he held it much longer than I expected him to.

"What do you want from me, Kozart?"

"What do you mean?"

"Why am I here?"

He shrugged.

"That's not an answer."

He held my gaze again.

I tried to read the thoughts playing across his face. Tried to decipher why we'd ended up there together. Why he kept contacting me if he didn't want sex.

"I guess I wasn't ready to watch you walk away yet."

An unexpected ripple rolled through my belly. "You're the one who walked away after the wedding."

"I didn't have a choice."

I lowered myself down onto the edge of the bed. "When are you going to be honest with me?"

"About what?"

I cocked my head. A silent plea for him to be truthful.

He crossed his arms and leaned against the wall. "I just need to know I can trust you."

"Trust me?"

He nodded. "I *want* to trust you."

"So, is this some type of test?"

He shook his head but shrugged at the same time, as if he wasn't even sure.

"Is there a reason you want to trust me?"

He shrugged again.

"Do you have a hard time trusting people?"

He paused for a long time then nodded.

"Well, the way I see it, you can either trust me or not. That's more on you than it is on me."

Though his eyes never wavered from mine, he said nothing for a long stretch.

I was beginning to see a pattern with these long bouts of silence. He was either taking in what I said or he was hoping I kept talking so he didn't have to.

"I liked kissing you," he finally said.

I swallowed hard, all coherent thoughts grinding to a halt. "Oh?"

"And I liked sleeping next to you."

My lips parted, and I suddenly found it impossible to speak.

"I don't usually sleep well," he admitted, his hands suddenly fidgeting with one another. "That night and the nights I've spoken to you, I've slept like a rock. The only thing I can figure is you play some part in that."

My forehead creased as the elated haze cleared and his words actually registered. "So, I'm here because you think I help you sleep?"

He winced. "When you say it like that, I sound like a dick."

"No. I'm just…not sure if I should be flattered or scared."

His eyes flashed away. I could see it was just as awkward for him to admit it to me as it was for me to have to hear it.

What the hell had I gotten myself into? And why did I feel so let down by his admission?

"Is that why you wanted my picture? So you could fall asleep?"

He lifted his shoulder. "I figured it could help."

I let out a shaky breath.

"If you wanna leave, I totally get it," he said.

I did want to leave. And I did feel let down. But I wasn't about to let my bruised ego stand in the way of helping out the guy who not too long ago came to my rescue. "Where's this T-shirt you promised me?" I tried to sound unfazed and upbeat, but it totally blew. "Let's get you to sleep."

Relief washed over Kozart's face as he moved to his suitcase and pulled out some obscure band T-shirt. "Sorry it's not a country band T-shirt."

I stood from the bed and plucked the T-shirt from his hand. "Be right back."

I disappeared into the bathroom. As soon as I was alone, I dropped onto the edge of the tub, needing a minute to process what just occurred. For the second time in a month, I was in a hotel room with a rock star and nothing was going to happen between us.

I had to be the lamest person on the freaking planet.

But what did I expect?

Why would some rock star want me—other than to sleep—when he could have any celebrity he wanted? Clearly, all he had to do was snap his fingers, and he was given what he wanted.

I closed my eyes and pinched the bridge of my nose. He'd helped me when I needed it. And, as crazy as his request was, I couldn't desert him when he needed me because my pride was hurt.

I yanked off my top and bra and tugged his T-shirt over my head. It smelled like him. It was odd that I already knew his soapy scent, but I did. I slipped off my jeans and stood, folding my clothes into a pile. After using the bathroom and washing my hands, I put some of Kozart's toothpaste on my finger and brushed my teeth. Once I was done, I pulled in a deep breath and walked out of the bathroom.

Kozart sat on the bed with his back against the headboard, and his jean-clad legs stretched out in front of him. He'd even removed his hat. He *was* gorgeous. He glanced up from his phone which he held in his hand. His eyes widened as they moved from my bare feet to his T-shirt hanging down to my bare thighs. "Rock looks good on you."

I smirked, wondering what a *rock star* would look like on me.

Virtual palm to forehead.

I *was* the lamest person on the planet.

I walked to the dresser and placed my clothes down before turning to him. He patted the space beside him, and as if he had this magical pull, I moved to the right side of the bed. He lifted the sheets and I slipped under, turning on my side and propping myself up on my elbow. "Aren't you getting under?"

"Not yet...You really only listen to country music?" he asked.

"Yup. Love me some southern boys."

"You know I live in Nashville."

"I kind of remember you saying that."

He smirked but said nothing.

"So, where's my picture? By your bed?"

His face sobered. "Are you making fun of me?"

Shit. "No. I'm sorry. It sucks you can't sleep."

"I wish I could. I've tried everything. Some things I'm embarrassed to admit, but nothing worked, until..."

"That passed-out girl you stumbled upon in a bar?"

"You weren't passed out," he reminded me.

I smirked, loving that he remembered our conversation as vividly as I did.

He frowned. "I know it sounds fucked up. *I* sound fucked up. And maybe I am. But can we just see what happens?"

My heart squeezed in my chest. "You can call me any time, you know? Even FaceTime if you'd like to see this smiling face." I smiled wide, flashing all my teeth for effect.

He laughed.

"Why do you think you can't sleep?"

His laughter subsided and silence filled the room. I figured I'd hit on a sore subject.

"You don't have to tell me if you don't want to," I said, trying to give him a way out.

"No, it's fine." But he said nothing else for a long time. "I grew up bouncing around the foster system."

"I'm sorry. That had to be tough."

"I never knew what I'd get in every new placement...Would the father be a drunk? The wife a pill freak? The kids vindictive and out to make my life hell? I had to sleep with one eye open at all times."

I closed my eyes, willing back the tears that pricked them.

"Since then, I haven't been able to sleep. I get a few hours here and there, mostly interrupted, but..." He shrugged. "What can you do?"

Now it made sense why he'd never been brought to a speech pathologist for his stuttering. He never had parents who looked out for his well-being. He had temporary placements and no real ties. "What happened to your real parents?"

His lips twisted and his eyes averted mine.

Had I asked too many questions? Pushed him too far?

He finally looked back to me. "Between stints in prison and dealing and doing drugs, they weren't fit to raise a kid."

I said nothing, hoping he felt comfortable enough to tell me more.

"Between the strangers in and out of our apartment to the days I'd go without food, being in foster care was a dream compared to the shit I went through with them."

"I'm sorry you grew up that way."

He said nothing more.

The urge to comfort him overwhelmed me. "At least someday you can give your own children the things you didn't have. Two parents. A stable home. A—"

"Skateboard."

"A skateboard?" I asked.

"I never had a skateboard," he admitted. "And I always wanted one."

I lay there, not knowing what to say. Imagine this grown man still remembering something he wanted as a kid and couldn't have.

"I probably would've fallen on my ass, but I always saw kids riding them, and I just wanted one so bad."

"A best friend necklace," I said. "The one where you get one side of the heart and your best friend gets the other side. I always wanted one of those."

"See? No one's life is perfect," he said. "And there's no measure for what hurts us. Hurt is hurt. And disappointment is disappointment. They're what make us who we are." He climbed off the bed and pulled down his jeans, leaving him in black boxer briefs. I knew it probably wasn't the time to check him out after he'd admitted something so big, but *Yum*. He climbed under the sheets and lay on his back beside me.

"What? No spooning?" I asked, trying to change the mood in the room.

"I'm not sure I need that," he said, not being rude just honest.

"Well, maybe I do." I turned away from him and lay on my side, trying not to feel sorry for myself while waiting to see what he did next.

The bed moved and I could feel him twist. I smiled as his arms slipped around me and he buried his nose in my hair. His scent wrapped itself around me and I released a silent breath.

"See? Not so bad," I said.

"Thanks."

I said nothing, just lay there realizing how screwed up we were. Him needing me to sleep. Me *knowing* he only needed me to sleep, but staying there nonetheless.

And what happened if it didn't work? What happened if it was all in his head? Would he be done with me? Would I be okay with that?

"Your ex was an idiot," he said.

"I know."

"Do you? Because, look at you. You're gorgeous and you're taking pity on a pervy stalker who tells you he needs you to sleep."

I laughed to myself, knowing there was no way I'd be doing this with some pervy stalker. Half the world knew who Kozart Z Savage was. That somehow made him safe. "What'd you say? I missed what came after you called me gorgeous."

His whole body shook with silent laughter. He pulled me tighter against his chest, and I hated that I liked it. Hated that a single compliment rendered me incapable of feeling bitter toward him for not wanting me.

Silence surrounded us for a long time.

I focused on Kozart's steady breathing. On the way my body fit with his. On the way I felt so at ease in his arms.

Those were my last thoughts before I drifted off to sleep in the arms of a rock star who was slowly letting his walls down around me. And I wished I could stop myself from liking it.

CHAPTER NINE

Kozart

I woke from a dead-to-the-world sleep to the feel of a soft back pressed to my chest. The subtle smell of rose petals floated off her skin—the same silky skin barely covered by my T-shirt.

I'd fucked up last night.

I'd told Aubrey way more about me than I intended. But there was something about her that caused me to say too much.

I hadn't been lying, though. Her presence eased me. It helped me relax. It helped me sleep. I didn't have to worry she was taking off with something of mine to sell online while I slept. I didn't have to worry she was taking pictures of us in bed together to post on social media. That's not who she was, and I knew it the moment we met.

She shifted in my arms, and the T-shirt I'd lent her skated up as her ass pressed against me.

I was definitely not a saint. And my body reacted to her the way it would to any other hot female. But I didn't want to scare her off so I slowly shifted, trying to move my dick away from her ass.

"Morning," she breathed, her voice raspy.

"Morning."

"Did you sleep?" she asked.

"I did."

She relaxed on a sigh. "Good."

Had she been worried I wouldn't?

"There's something to be said for spooning, huh?" she said.

"Who would've known?"

She laughed.

"You hungry?"

"Not really."

Disappointment filled me in an unfamiliar way. I told her the previous night I wanted to show her something, but had I blown it when I told her the real reason I wanted her there? "Do you have plans today?"

"Not sure. Some guy told me he had something to show me."

"You make a habit of looking at things guys want to show you?" I asked her.

"Depends."

"Well, I do have something I'd like you to see."

"Is this where you go and get all pervy on me?"

I laughed. "No. I have some*where* I'd like to take you."

"Oh."

Was that an oh, good? Or oh, I can't get away from this guy fast enough? "I can take you home so you can shower and get changed first."

"You think I want you to know where I live?" she asked like the smartass I was beginning to see she was.

"You *have* slept with me twice."

She chuckled.

"So, is that a yes?"

"Maybe."

"Maybe? Are you gonna make me beg?"

"I'm curious what that would look like."

Oh, this girl. "Please will you join me this afternoon, Aubrey?"

"You've got to do better than that."

I stifled a smile as I racked my brain for something better to entice her. "There's something I haven't told you and I'd like to tell you today."

"Why can't you just tell me now?"

"I want to show you."

She exhaled a long dramatic breath. "Okay."

"That's it?"

"Yup. I'm easy."

Oh, she was far from easy. And for some reason, I really liked that.

* * *

We slipped out the staff entrance to a waiting car. I wore my ball cap. Aubrey had her jeans back on, was still wearing my T-shirt, and carried her shoes from the night before in her hand. She gave my driver, Arthur, her address and we settled into the backseat, comfortably silent. She stared out the window at the passing buildings, and I wondered what she was thinking about. What she thought I wanted to show her. What she'd *think* when I told her my secret.

She turned to look at me. "I need to warn you about something."

My eyes shifted to hers.

"My roommate may interrogate you. I forgot to let her know I wouldn't be home last night."

"She wasn't out with you?"

"No, it's not her scene."

The car pulled to a stop in front of Aubrey's condo a short while later. From the street, I could see it was a well-maintained townhouse with a sidewalk that ran up the center of the front lawn.

My driver stepped out and opened the door for us.

"Thanks," Aubrey said to him as she stepped out, not seeming to question the fact that I had a driver.

I climbed out behind her. "This looks nice." I spotted some students walking nearby and grabbed hold of her hand, leading her toward the house a little faster than necessary with my head down. I didn't want to be seen on campus. Things like that had happened before, and before I knew it, crowds had gathered out front waiting for me to leave.

Fucking internet.

Once inside, I released Aubrey's hand and followed her to the second floor. She unlocked the door and we stepped inside her condo. It was small, but clean. I'd seen my fair share of dumps growing up in the system, and this place was clean and maintained for a rental.

Aubrey searched the condo for her roommate, but since it was pretty small, her search ended quickly. "Looks like you're safe. She's not here."

"No interrogation?"

"No interrogation." She gestured toward the sofa. "Make yourself at home. I'll just be a few minutes."

"No rush. Take your time."

She disappeared down the hall looking hot in my T-shirt. *Fuck.* I shouldn't have been having those thoughts about her. I needed her. I didn't need to fuck her.

I heard the shower switch on in the bathroom a few minutes later, so I grabbed the remote and flipped on the television. After finding nothing that held my interest, my curiosity got the best of me. I stood and crept down the hallway, glancing into the first room I stumbled upon. The walls were dark red and the comforter black. Nope. Not Aubrey's room.

I glanced to the room across the hall and found an airy white room with a teal comforter. *This* looked like Aubrey. I walked inside, feeling like a creepy stalker. Pictures were tucked into the frame of her mirror. Her

with three blondes. Wait. Triplets. Talk about every guy's fantasy. And while her friends were undoubtedly hot, Aubrey, with her long dark waves, was beautiful without even trying.

"What the hell?!"

I spun around, expecting to see Aubrey in a towel. But a short raven-haired girl wearing big black combat boots stood there with wide eyes.

Her mouth gaped. "Why are you here?"

"I'm with Aubrey," I explained.

"No. Why is Z *Savage* in my roommate's bedroom?"

"First of all, she has no idea who I am, so I'd really like to keep it that way for a little while longer. And two, I'm taking her out today and she's just getting ready."

She stared across the room at me as if in some sort of trance. "I love you."

I chuckled. "You don't know me."

"I love your music," she explained.

"Thank you. I work hard on those songs."

"I was at your show this summer. It was *amazing.* 'Moonlight' is my all-time favorite song. Thank you for singing it in the encore."

"I'm glad you liked it."

"Can I maybe get an autograph?"

"Sure." My eyes cut toward the door. The shower still ran in the bathroom. "But can we hurry? I really don't want Aubrey to know yet."

"She hates rock music," she explained.

"I know. I'm hoping she at least likes mine a little."

"She usually asks me to turn it down."

I laughed to myself as she hurried off to her room. Of course, Aubrey asked her to turn down my music. Of course, she'd be the one girl unfazed by me.

Her roommate returned with an actual album of my first record and a black marker.

"You've got it in vinyl?" I asked.

"Of course."

I laughed as I took both from her, checking out the mint condition of the album cover. The empty fish bowl had been symbolic at the time. Now? Not so much.

"What's your name?" I asked.

"Eliza with an E."

I signed the album: *To Eliza, Thanks for loving the music. Z*

"This will be our little secret," she winked as she took the album and marker from me.

"Thanks."

"Are you going to our show tonight?"

She shook her head. "It sold out in five minutes."

"I can leave you tickets at the will-call window if you'd like to go. Because it's sold out, the seats might be in the nose-bleed section, but..."

"I'll be there," Eliza assured me, visibly trying to hold back her excitement.

"I'm gonna head back out there before Aubrey finds me in here."

She nodded.

I returned to my spot on the sofa just as the water in the shower switched off.

"Give me ten minutes," Aubrey called as she scurried out of the bathroom and into her room.

I listened to see if Eliza snuck in and gave me away, but she didn't. I took that time to text my manager and had him set aside two tickets for her.

Ten minutes later, Aubrey stepped out in jeans and a white cami with a black fitted jacket over it. My T-shirt was in her hand. "Want me to wash it?"

looked to me first. "What would you like? And don't say salad or I'll have to let you out right here."

I rarely ate meat, but there was no way I was letting his salad theory win. "Double cheeseburger with just mustard. And a diet soda."

He smiled and ordered, adding a drink and two burgers for himself before rolling up his window.

The driver pulled forward and paid the cashier. He grabbed our food and handed it back to us before driving off.

"Anywhere secluded around here to eat outside?" Kozart asked.

"My stalker antennae just went up."

He laughed. "Or we could just drive around and eat."

"Whatever you want."

He reached into the bag and grabbed my burger, handing it to me before calling up to the driver. "Would you mind putting some country music on?"

The driver obliged, turning on some modern country.

"You really like this?" Kozart asked as the country music drifted through the speakers.

"Love it," I said with a mouthful of burger.

"Why?"

I shrugged. "I love mellow music. Music with a story. Music that speaks to me and I can relate to."

He nodded. "So, you like sappy love songs."

"Well, *yeah*. But I also like fun party music. What about you?"

"I like most music."

"But not country?"

He shrugged. "I'd be willing to give it a chance."

"So, when do I get to see the surprise."

He smirked, that I-know-something-you-don't-know look in his eyes. "Soon."

I nibbled on my burger before asking, "You said you live in Nashville?"

"When I'm in town."

"How often are you in town?"

He shrugged. "Have *you* always lived in Tennessee?"

"Yup."

"Do you plan to stay once you graduate?"

"I still need to get my master's degree, so I'll be around here for at least two more years."

"You'll make a good speech pathologist," he said.

"How do you know?"

"You're patient."

I scoffed. "That you know of."

"You're kind."

"Unless you piss me off."

He laughed.

A few minutes later we pulled into the parking lot of the city's concert arena. Our driver drove us around back to where eighteen wheelers and tour buses were parked.

My eyes shot to Kozart's, expecting him to spill the beans. But he just gave me an almost apologetic smile. And for the first time since meeting him, he seemed anxious. Nervous even.

He wiped his mouth with a napkin and grabbed his drink, sipping it down.

The car stopped at a back entrance. The driver stepped out of the car, circled around, and opened my door. Kozart lifted his chin, urging me out. I abandoned my half-eaten food which he discarded in his bag. I stepped out and he joined me, leading us to the door and pounding twice with the side of his fist.

The same big man who'd let us into the hotel pushed open this door.

"What's up, man?" Kozart said to him as he led me inside.

"Hi," I said, earning myself a nod from the big man.

My heart drummed faster as we moved down a long, deserted hallway. This was it. Did I pretend I didn't know? Was he waiting to see my surprised reaction? We reached an entryway at the end of the hallway. It opened to a small set of stairs leading up to a huge stage.

Kozart turned to me, excitement beaming from his eyes. "I know you're not into rock music, but I'm hoping you'll give my band a try."

I stared at him, unable to tear my eyes away from the hope they held.

"I've got to do a sound check, but you can sit right in front."

"Okay."

He led me to another entryway that brought us out to the main floor of the arena. The space was filled with endless rows of empty seats. I twisted around, taking in the over twenty-thousand seats that would be filled for Kozart's show which I assumed was later that night.

"I should have told you sooner."

I twisted to face him. "So, you have a show tonight?"

He nodded. "I'd love for you to come to it."

"Let me hear this sound check, then I'll decide."

He smiled.

"Yo, Z? You ready, man?" a guy on stage called.

Kozart spun around to find his drummer behind the drums and his guitarist wrapping his strap around his shoulders. "Yeah. Gimme a minute." He looked back to me. "This is probably a little overwhelming."

"I'm not calling you Z."

His smirk slid into place. "I wouldn't want you to…" He leveled me with serious eyes. "Please just have an open mind."

I nodded as he took off for the stage. I dropped into the nearest seat and watched as he stepped to center stage and adjusted the microphone stand. He motioned to his band, including another guitarist who'd just joined them, and they began to play. The acoustics in the arena were loud but crisp. My knees bounced with anticipation as I sat in the front row. I'd heard his songs, but would I like them more in person?

The song's instrumental intro music seemed to be subsiding which meant Kozart would sing. And he did. His deep raspy voice echoed through the arena. He didn't look at me when he sang. He just gripped the microphone and leaned in, belting the lyrics to one of their heaviest songs. The drums reverberated throughout the room. The bass pounded, almost hurting my ears. And Kozart sang. Boy, did he sing.

The song eventually ended, and he spoke to the guys at the control board on the opposite end of the arena, noting adjustments they needed to make before the night's performance. His eyes flashed to mine. "Since I have a special guest with me who prefers mellower music," he announced, "I'd like to slow it down and play 'Second Act.'"

His band started up with a slower, softer accompaniment. The music sounded unfamiliar. I wondered if it was new and not yet released. Kozart's eyes drifted shut and he sang a beautiful rock ballad about getting another chance at love—a second act that was so much sweeter than the first.

"I love her," Treyton shouted as we moved away from them.

Kozart rolled his eyes as we stepped through the door which the big bodyguard held open for us.

"Thanks Reggie," Kozart said.

I smiled my thanks to him, yet he said nothing as we disappeared between the rows of buses and trucks. "So, this is quite the life."

"It's something," Kozart said.

As we approached the tour bus, he pushed on the door and we climbed inside. The empty bus was bigger than it looked on the outside, with a sitting area behind the driver's seat. A small kitchen with granite counters and stainless-steel appliances sat across from it, and bunk beds ran down both sides of the aisle.

"My bedroom's in the back," Kozart explained as he rested against the counter and crossed his arms.

"You drew the long stick?" I asked with a raised brow.

He shrugged.

"You should give the other guys the bedroom once in a while."

He scoffed. "I tell you I can't sleep, and you want me to give up my room?"

"Switch things up. You never know what'll happen."

"Yeah," he said, his eyes absorbing the details of my face. "I'm starting to see that."

I dropped into a seat, the implication behind his words turning my knees to putty. "So, why rock?"

"I needed it when I was younger," he admitted. "The anger in the lyrics. The release of pain. It was an outlet for me and it just stuck."

"You could try a little country."

He laughed. "Could you see me in cowboy boots?"

"They don't all wear boots. A lot of them even wear ball caps if you can believe that?"

"I don't."

I laughed.

"Will you be honest with me?" Kozart asked, pushing off the counter and sitting down beside me. "Did you know who I was before I brought you here?"

I chewed on my bottom lip, feeling like a big fat liar for not telling him sooner.

"You did," he said with disappointment in his eyes.

"Why didn't you just tell me?" I asked.

He shrugged. "I'm so fucking sick of people treating me different because I'm a…"

"Rock star?"

His eyes averted mine.

"If it's any consolation, I had no idea who you were at the wedding. My sister told me the next day."

"I *knew* she knew. I could see it in her eyes."

"Sorry to disappoint, but your name meant nothing to me when she told me."

"Did you troll me once you knew?"

I laughed. "Troll you? No. I saw a few pictures and felt like I was invading your privacy."

"You never called me," he said. "After I called you and you had my number."

"Why would I call you?"

He shrugged. "Most girls would give anything for their shot with a rock star."

"I'm not most girls." I bumped him with my shoulder. "And I'm not impressed by rock stars."

He grinned. "Of course, you're not."

"So…why Z? Where'd that come from?"

"Ko-Zzzzart."

"I knew that."

He chuckled. "It's not that original. Just something Treyton used to call me."

My brows climbed. "Used to?"

"I met him in my last foster home when we were both seventeen." A wave of nostalgia swept over his features. "I'm thinking we were their last foster kids."

"That bad?"

"That bad."

I laughed, imagining a teenage Kozart. "What about the other guys?"

"Met them at an open mic night when I was eighteen. Our sounds just naturally jived."

I nodded, understanding what it was like to have an unspoken connection to someone else. "So, when do you leave?"

"Right after the show," he said, a glint of regret in his eyes.

My insides mirrored that feeling, and I scolded myself for allowing it to. This wasn't like that. We weren't like that. He'd made that clear last night. "Well, this concert better be amazing."

"So, you're coming?"

I feigned boredom. "If I must."

"Well, just so you know. I didn't plan to let you leave until I was on this bus heading out of town."

"Stalker."

* * *

The girls beside me in the front row stood on their chairs, their cropped tops lifting to their boobs as they danced and sang every song at the tops of their lungs. I stood there, taking in the music, the people around me, and the buzz of excitement electrifying the arena. The arena shook with cheers, echoed with applause, and buzzed with the sex appeal Kozart exuded in every note he sang. Sweat dripped down his face as he held the last note of the song for an exuberant amount of time. The place erupted. I could feel the reverberation in my fingertips and toes.

Once the song ended, Kozart grabbed a towel off a nearby speaker and wiped his face. He turned and tossed it to the crowd. A swarm of fans lunged for it. I knew people loved him, but this was insanity.

His eyes cut to mine and he flashed that knowing smirk. The girls beside me squealed, clearly thinking it was intended for them. I kinda liked knowing it was for me. Liked knowing I knew a piece of him they'd never know.

"I've recently been trying to convert a friend of mine from country to rock," Kozart told the audience, his image on the screen behind the stage making him larger than life.

The crowd screamed their concurrence.

"Now this friend is convinced country is the only genre of music that tells a story. That connects to you. That talks of love."

The crowd went wild and the girls beside me screamed, "We love you, Z!"

I rolled my eyes, unable to take the dramatics he was obviously creating for my benefit.

He laughed and I knew that, too, was directed at me.

"Why don't we show this friend how wrong she is?" he yelled.

The place went crazy as the music for his next song began.

Every girl around me screamed. And all I could do was sit back and enjoy the show.

* * *

The lights were on and the seats had emptied out. A few fans lingered. Reggie approached me, motioning over with his head. I followed him to the door by the stage I'd used earlier, unsure what I'd find backstage.

But what I found were Kozart's band members eating food and talking to people I hadn't seen earlier. There were a few girls sitting together on the sofa, giggling and playing on their phones. Their tight clothes and giddiness told me they were brought backstage from the concert. Was that what Kozart did? Did he select girls from the crowd to warm his bed and help him pass the time before a few hours of sleep hopefully pulled him under?

"Aubrey."

I twisted to the sound of Kozart's voice. He stepped through the doorway, freshly showered and in a clean T-shirt. I pulled in a sharp breath, wishing I wasn't trying so hard to freeze the moment in my brain. To memorize his knowing smirk. His wet tussled hair. His confident stride.

It was only a matter of minutes before he'd be taking off for Alabama where he had a show the following night.

He grasped hold of my arm and led me away from prying eyes, through another doorway and into a vacant hallway. "What'd you think?"

"You want honesty or what everyone else would tell you?" I asked.

"Honesty."

"It was good. *You* were good. I was surprised the girls beside me were able to keep their tops on for the entire show."

He chuckled, but his eyes dodged mine.

A long stretch of silence passed between us. We both knew he was leaving. But where did that leave us?

"So…" I finally said.

"So," he said, looking up at me through his long eyelashes.

I didn't know what to say. I wanted more time with him. I wanted him to want to stay longer. But that wasn't what this was. "You gonna be able to sleep tonight?"

"I sure hope so. If not, expect a call."

I smiled.

He stepped forward and wrapped his arms around me, pulling me into a hug.

I breathed him in, committing his just-showered scent to memory.

"I'm glad I ran into you," he said into my hair.

"Which time?"

He paused. "Both." He released me and stepped back. He stared down at me, lifting his hand to my cheek and grazing his fingertips over it gently.

My heartbeat began to race. I leaned into his touch.

He leaned closer and dropped his forehead to mine. He paused for a long moment. "I want to kiss you so fucking bad right now."

My breath caught in my throat.

"But that would be promising you something I can't give," he said.

My entire body wilted. He had to have felt it. "Is that what those girls back there are about?"

He pulled back, his eyes narrowed. "What?"

"You can sleep with them and never see them again and you're both good with that?"

"You think I'm heading back in there to fuck some groupies?"

"Isn't that what rock stars do?"

A giggling girl and Treyton burst out of the room we'd been in. "Oops," Treyton said, taking the girl by the hand and slipping inside another room.

"Fuck," Kozart hissed, knowing Treyton had proven my point. "You had a guy cheat on you, Aubrey," he said. "I'm not leaving you here thinking this is something it isn't."

I nearly choked on my shock. He'd never spoken to me so harshly.

"If I kiss you right now, that's promising you something. And I can't do that and then go sleep with some groupie. And I *will* sleep with some groupie. It's inevitable."

"That's funny. I thought you only sleep with me," I countered.

"Dammit," he hissed. "I fuck groupies. I don't sleep with them. I was telling you the truth when I said it only happens with you."

Tears glossed my vision. I was so stupid. Why did I keep forgetting that all I was to him was a sleep aid? A distraction from his screwed-up sleep. I pulled in a breath and wore a reassuring grin. "It's fine, Kozart. I get it."

I could've sworn he growled deep in his throat as I stepped away from him.

"I should get going."

"My driver's gonna bring you back to your place."

I nodded.

Our gazes locked for a long time. We both had things we wanted to say, but what was the point? He was leaving and I was staying. And like he said, there was nothing to promise me.

"Thanks for a great weekend. I'll be sure to post all about it online," I said, incapable of not being a smartass.

His gaze dropped from mine. "Liar."

"Bye, Kozart."

He said nothing, just wore a sad smile as I turned away from him and walked to the back exit.

As I slipped into the backseat of the waiting car, I held my breath, willing away any foolish tears that threatened to fall. I looked straight ahead, berating myself for hoping he'd run out and stop the car.

The engine started and the car pulled away from the arena with Kozart Savage still inside with his bandmates and some groupies who he'd all but assured me he'd be fucking.

* * *

"Oh. My. Freaking. God," Eliza said, nearly tackling me when I walked inside our condo twenty minutes later. "You spent the night with Z *freaking* Savage. Please tell me you had sex with him. *Please.*"

"I did not." I slipped my black jacket off and tossed it on the chair.

She exhaled dramatically as she dropped down onto the sofa. "Why the hell not?"

"Because we're…friends…kind of."

"Girl, you need to dish right now and put me out of my misery."

I moved to the recliner chair and sat. "I met him at the bar in the hotel at my sister's wedding. But I didn't know who he was."

Eliza's mouth hung open. "Do you live under a rock?"

I shrugged. "I listen to country."

"Doesn't mean you can't appreciate some gorgeous eye candy."

I rolled my eyes.

"So?" she prodded.

"So, he showed up at the bar Friday night."

"That's no coincidence," she said.

I shrugged. "We ended up back at his hotel and we just slept."

She dramatically dropped her head back against the sofa and groaned.

"It is what it is," I assured her.

"I don't buy it."

"He's leaving and I'm here."

She looked unconvinced, but I didn't want to break her heart about her rock god who was currently getting action with some groupie.

"Listen, you can't tell anyone about this."

She nodded. "I'm good at keeping secrets."

"I'm not even telling the triplets. I don't want *anyone* knowing."

She held up her hands in surrender. "Whatever you want. But just tell me you at least kissed him."

I shook my head. "Just at my sister's wedding, but that was only to make Geoffrey jealous."

"Wow," she mused. "Z freaking Savage and *my* roommate. I am so damn jealous."

"There's nothing to be jealous about."

"I was at the show," Eliza admitted.

"What?"

"When you were in the shower, he said he'd leave me tickets at the arena."

"Why didn't you tell me?"

"He said he wanted to come clean with you first. I wasn't sure if he had."

I dragged in a deep breath, unsure what to think. It was as if he was two different people—a thoughtful guy who hooked my friend up with tickets and a guy living the rock star life—and all that entailed. I stood up. "I'm gonna go to bed. Goodnight."

"Night," she called as I walked into the bathroom to wash up and brush my teeth.

A few minutes later, I stepped into my room and closed the door behind me. I sat on the edge of my bed, exhausted. I slipped out my phone and checked it for the umpteenth time. Nothing. I hadn't actually expected him to call or text. I assumed he was busy with the groupies before taking off for Alabama. My stomach roiled at the thought, and I hated myself for getting so swept up in him so quickly.

I stood and moved to my dresser. As I took off my watch and jewelry, I remembered I had a couple tests the upcoming week. I'd totally let school flee from my brain. It was easy being caught up in Kozart's world and forgetting everything else.

A soft knock came from my door. Eliza probably wanted to know if I got his autograph for her. Little did she know I was getting the blow-off to top all blow-offs. "Come in."

My door swung open and Kozart stood there, his eyes burning into mine from across the room.

My heartbeat began to thrash in my chest.

He slammed the door behind him and stalked toward me. I froze as he stepped in front of me and his hands cupped my cheeks. He stared down into my eyes. "I'm a fucking idiot." His lips crashed down on mine. His tongue thrust between my lips and he devoured my mouth in the most delicious way possible. I could barely keep up. His lips moved fast and possessively. His tongue danced with mine.

I slipped my arms around his neck and arched into him. He grabbed my ass and lifted me right off my feet. My legs wrapped around his hips as he carried me to the bed, laying me down and covering me with his body. His elbows rested beside my head as his fingers tunneled through my hair, his lips still moving in sync with mine. Heat shot to my core as my heartbeat raced. His lips deserted mine, leaving us both breathless. He dropped his mouth to my shoulder and assaulted my collarbone with open-mouthed kisses. "God, you taste so good."

I dropped my head back, giving him better access.

"Watching you walk away…" he said between kisses, "…was like a fucking dagger to my heart."

My hands drifted up his back. "Is that a line from one of your songs?"

He chuckled before pulling back so he could look at me. "No, but maybe it should be."

I laughed, loving having him on top of me, looking just as turned on as I was.

"I needed to kiss you right, Aubrey. I needed to be sure no kiss would ever compare."

My brow shot up. "What happened to no promises?"

"We both know I was lying out of my ass."

I tried to stifle a smile, but I was so damn happy I couldn't. "So, what now?"

"Oh, I have plenty of ideas," he said before dropping a slow kiss to my lips.

My hands ran under the back of his shirt, my fingertips trailing over his smooth skin and corded muscles.

He eventually pulled away, his lips wet with my kiss. "Can I stay here tonight?"

"What about Alabama?"

"My driver said he'd drive me in the morning."

I stared into his eyes, the same eyes that had only half an hour before sent me away. "Does this mean you're gonna stop being afraid?"

He cocked his head. "Of what?"

"Of letting people in. It's why you tried to push me away tonight."

His gaze lowered from mine.

"I get it. It's easier if you're the one leaving other people behind," I said. "It's what happened to you all your life."

His gaze met mine. "Then why'd you leave?"

"You were acting like a dick."

He laughed at my candor. "I was trying to be honest with you. I've lived the last five years in different places most nights. I get lonely. I have sex with girls. I'm not proud of it. And I won't lie and say I don't enjoy it. It's just the way it's been. I can't promise you I won't be with someone else. I don't want to be that guy that makes empty promises because I know it could happen. And knowing that makes me want to warn you up front. And not take it somewhere it shouldn't go."

I nodded, trying to ignore the hollowness in my chest his honesty created.

He twisted a wave of my hair around his finger. "I like who I am with you. And I like that you're someone who makes me feel like maybe there are people out there I can trust. I need you in my life, Aubrey."

I stared at him, scared to say a word.

"I want to sleep with you tonight," he said. "*Just* sleep."

I rolled my eyes. "Don't worry about my ego or anything."

He smirked. "I want to text you every day and talk to you every night. I don't want to ruin anything by having sex. Sex makes everything more complicated."

"Not with your groupies."

"Because they know the score."

I hated myself in that moment. I'd just gotten out of a relationship with a guy who wanted to hide his cheating. Now I was disappointed that a guy who was telling me he'd sleep around didn't want to sleep with me. *Classic. Truly classic.*

"Let's see what this thing is between us," he said, sincerity emanating from his blue eyes. "Can we do that?"

I wanted to believe he needed me like he said he did, but I'd been played for a fool before. And I wouldn't be that oblivious girl again. But spending time with a rock star, one I was slowly developing feelings for, would be a surefire way to ensure oblivion. I wouldn't know what or who he was doing while he was away. After what happened with Geoffrey, I didn't know if I had the capacity to give someone that much of my trust. Especially when he was telling me he didn't trust himself.

"You want honesty?" I asked.

He nodded.

"Then I don't know."

"That's fair," he said, as if it's the answer he expected. "I just laid a lot out on the table for you." He cupped my cheek and his eyes assessed my face for a long time, like he'd never actually looked at me before. "You're so beautiful."

"You're so full of shit."

He laughed. "Usually. But not with you. With you I give it to you straight. Probably because you don't fall at my feet."

"Does it ever get old? Living the rock star life?"

"Hearing the words I wrote sung back to me each night by over twenty thousand fans is fucking amazing. And hearing people scream my name like I'm God's gift to the world ain't bad either." He laughed a humorless laugh. "But the truth is, those fans don't know me. They only know what they hear in my lyrics, or what I say in interviews, or what they think they know by looking at my life."

"Sounds bittersweet."

"The good outweighs the bad, and I'd never wanna sound like an ungrateful bastard because these fans have given me a damn good life. But you wanted the truth, so there it is."

"Thanks for being honest."

He shrugged like it was no big deal. But it was. Everything he shared just made me know him more. And trust him more. He leaned down and sucked on my bottom lip.

The area between my legs quivered as my eyelids fluttered shut. But he didn't kiss me. He tugged my bottom lip gently with his teeth before moving to my top lip. He sucked on it before licking his way underneath to my gums. I'd never had a guy do that before and the numbness that ensued brought on a throbbing between my legs. What the hell was he doing to me? "Kozart," I groaned.

"Yes?"

"I like that."

He chuckled. "I bet I could find a lot of things you—"

My bedroom door flew open.

Kozart and I both sprang up.

The triplets stood in my doorway, their mouths gaping open.

"What the hell?" Melinda said.

"Holy shit," Marla said.

"Oh my God," Mandy said.

My eyes widened as Kozart chuckled beside me. "What are you guys doing here?" Their clubbing outfits and unruly hair told me they'd been out partying all night.

"We were worried about you," Melinda said, staring at Kozart.

"You wouldn't return our texts after disappearing from the bar," Marla added.

"I guess we know why," Mandy said.

"I'm clearly fine."

Mandy's brows bounced. "We can see that."

"Can I call you tomorrow?" I asked, trying to get them out of my room.

They nodded, finally taking the hint. "Bye," they said, turning and hurrying out of the room.

I looked to Kozart as they giggled down the hallway. "I'm so sorry."

He shook his head like it wasn't a big deal.

I jumped up. "I'll be right back." I dashed out of my room and blocked the front door before they could leave. "Wait."

All three of them lipped, "Oh. My. *God.*"

I smiled, incapable of not. "Please don't tell anyone about this."

"Why not?" Marla asked.

"Because then word will spread and fans will be out there waiting to see him."

The realization of the situation flashed across their faces.

I leveled each of them with my eyes. "Please keep this quiet. I trust you guys."

"When he's gone," Mandy whispered. "You better tell us *everything*."

I nodded, hating that too many people were beginning to know about…whatever the hell this thing was between me and Kozart. And while I trusted the triplets, news like this might be too exciting for them not to share. I pulled open the door. "Thanks for checking on me. I love you guys."

"We love you, too," they said, before throwing their arms around me and hugging me.

As I closed the door behind them, I heard them giggling all the way down the stairs. I stood with my back against the door and closed my eyes for a long time, trying to calm my nerves.

"You okay?" Kozart asked.

My eyes popped open to find him standing in the hallway. "I'm so sorry. They were worried about me and—"

"Stop apologizing. You're lucky to have friends who care about you."

"Are you and your band tight like that?"

"I'd like to think so. But we're always one fight away from a tell-all book or interview happening."

I stared across the room realizing how hard it was to be him. To be able to trust people, but only so much. That had to suck.

I walked toward him, slipping my arms around him and looking up into his hypnotic blue eyes. "You said you *wanted* to trust me. You can."

He dropped a kiss on my head and turned us down the hallway.

"Goodnight, Eliza," I said as we walked by her closed door, knowing she'd let the triplets in.

"Goodnight you two," she called.

"I'll be right back," I said to Kozart, once I grabbed some clothes from my room and hurried into the bathroom.

I pulled off my jeans and slipped on my booty shorts. I tugged my cami and bra off and replaced them with a tank. The ribbed material did little to hide my pebbled nipples, thanks to the semi-naked rock star in my bed.

I moved back into my room, closing the door behind me. A ripple rolled through my body as Kozart sat on the edge of my bed in nothing but his black boxer briefs. I chewed on my bottom lip. No one had been in my bed in the last three years except Geoffrey, and he never looked that good in my space.

Kozart's eyes immediately dropped to my chest and he groaned. "How the hell am I gonna do this?"

I walked over to the bed and climbed under the sheets. "Do what?"

"Make it through the whole night with you looking like that?" he explained as he climbed underneath the sheets.

I turned on my side and propped myself up on my elbow. "Wouldn't be the first time we shared a bed with me looking like this."

He lay on his back laughing, the sweet sound filling my room.

"There is something to be said for making out."

"Is there?" Unexpectedly, Kozart turned toward me, spinning me onto my side away from him. He slipped his arms around me and pulled me flush against his chest.

"Ummm," I said, unsure why we weren't picking up where we left off before we were interrupted.

"I'm a firm believer in everything happening for a reason. Them barging in and stopping things from escalating was probably a good thing."

I scoffed.

He snickered. "We've got plenty of time, Aubrey."

Did we? Because by my calculation, he was leaving in less than eight hours. "Sleep well," I whispered into the darkness.

"I will," he assured me.

CHAPTER ELEVEN

Aubrey

I lay in bed with my phone in my hand and a rock star sound asleep beside me. My room was cloaked in semi-darkness, as the sun had yet to rise. I smiled with each song I added to a playlist I was creating for Kozart. I'd make him a country fan yet.

"What are you doing?" he whispered. "Come back and snuggle with me."

I placed my phone on my night stand and snuggled up against him.

He wrapped me in his arms and sighed. "Better."

"Careful. I might think you like snuggling more than spooning."

"With you I like them both."

I wanted to laugh, but the realization that he was leaving soon made it difficult. I breathed him in, the smooth skin of his chest like silk beneath my cheek. "Did you sleep well?"

"Do you even have to ask?"

I smiled into him. "So, I *do* have magic powers."

He chuckled softly.

"I was just making you something—not using my magic powers."

"Yeah?" he asked, surprised.

"I'll send it to you when you leave."

"Is it a naked picture of you?"

"What? God, no."

He laughed.

"Do girls send you naked pictures?"

"Not too many girls have my number. And the ones who do, wouldn't."

Hmm. Interesting.

"Who were the girls in the pictures with you at all those award shows?"

He shrugged. "Usually people my publicist or manager set me up with so people didn't think I was gay."

"Seriously?"

"Crazy, right?"

"That people would think you're gay?"

"No, that a rock god like me has to resort to being set up on dates."

"You did *not* just call yourself a rock god."

He rolled me over and covered me with his body. "Oh, but I did."

I shook my head, amused by his playfulness. "I guess it's better than heart throb."

"Oh, I've been called that before, too."

I dropped my head back and groaned. "It's shocking your head can even fit through the door."

He laughed.

When his laughter subsided, we lay in silence for a long time with his head on my chest and his arms wrapped around me. His heart beat in a steady rhythm. Music to my ears.

"What are you thinking?" he asked.

"Just if I'll pass my philosophy test now that a rock star consumed my time and attention this weekend."

"Liar."

I said nothing for a long time. "Do you write all your own songs?"

He nodded.

"Where do you get the ideas?"

He shrugged. "Life. Love. Loss. Girls who help me sleep."

I laughed. "Oh, you're good."

He chuckled. "I probably need to be going soon."

I nodded, knowing his departure was inevitable. "When will you be back in town?" I asked, trying not to sound needy.

"Not sure. I'll check my schedule and let you know."

"Does that mean I'll be graced by your presence again?"

"If you're lucky."

I laughed to myself.

"This sucks," he said, rolling off me and sitting on the edge of my bed.

I turned on my side and rested my cheek in my hand. "What?"

He glanced at me over his shoulder. "Leaving. I'm always leaving."

I sat up and traced the outline of the eagle tattoo on his back with my fingertip. The vast wings were detailed and shaded, giving it depth.

"I got that the day we got signed to our label," he explained.

"Why an eagle?"

"I know it's probably cliché, but I was finally free," he said.

My chest constricted, my heart aching for the boy who had shitty parents. The boy who saw too much and endured too much. The grown man he currently was who could trust very few people. "I'm so happy for you. You followed your dream and made something of yourself. You could've ended up so differently if you let yourself. And you didn't."

"From what you know," he countered.

"I'm a pretty good judge of character."

He twisted so he looked at me behind him. "So, what do you know?"

"I know…if I ripped my shirt off right now, you'd have a hard time resisting me."

His head dropped back and laughter poured out of him. "*Any* guy would have a hard time resisting you."

When his laughter subsided, he stood and put on the clothes he'd worn the previous night. "I'll be right back." He walked out of my room and I heard the bathroom door close.

I fell onto my stomach and buried my face in my pillow, trying to pull it together. He was leaving. He wasn't going to be loyal. He may or may not come back someday. *Ughhhhhh.*

I reached for my nightstand drawer and grabbed a piece of mint gum, popping it in my mouth—just in case.

The bathroom door opened and Eliza's giggle carried its way into my room as Kozart swept back in.

"Just ran into your roommate."

I chuckled to myself knowing she was *never* up this early. "I heard."

He shook his head, amused.

I climbed off the bed and walked to him, my toes touching his shoes.

He stared at me, the serious look in his eyes unsettling. "I'm usually not leaving anyone behind. I have no idea how to do this."

"Well…I still have a phone. I'll just be a phone call or text away. And when that doesn't work for you anymore, you need to let me know. Either way I'll be okay."

"I know you will." He pulled me into a hug and squeezed me in his arms. "I better do this here so I don't break your roommate's heart."

I tilted my head back so I could ask what he meant, but my words were cut off by his mouth crashing down on mine. His minty toothpaste-tasting tongue pushed its way into my mouth and he kissed me. Really kissed me. Head-moving-from-side-to-side, tongue-melding-with-mine kissed me. He pulled away only when he knew I'd be breathless. "Don't forget me."

I rolled my eyes while trying to control my breathing. "So dramatic."

He grabbed his ball cap off my dresser with a smirk and pulled it down low over his eyes.

"Disguise in place," I confirmed. "Let me walk you out. You wouldn't want Eliza to jump you or anything."

He followed me toward my bedroom door. I grabbed the handle, but his hand shot out and kept the door shut. He moved against my back so my chest pressed against the door. He lowered his lips to my shoulder and peppered the skin with soft kisses all the way up to my neck.

"Don't," I whispered as goosebumps scampered up my arms.

"Don't what?"

"Leave me wanting more."

An evil laugh escaped him. "Oh, babe, that's exactly what I'm doing."

I duck out from within his clutches and pulled open the door, more out of self-preservation than wanting to see him leave me.

He followed me down the hallway to the front door.

Eliza was curled up on the sofa watching television. "Leaving so soon?"

"Gotta be in 'Bama by noon," he explained. "It was great meeting you, Eliza."

I heard her breath hitch at the sound of her name on his lips. I totally understood the reaction. It happened to me, too. "You, too," she said. "And thanks again for the tickets."

I pulled open the front door. "Let me walk you down."

He followed me down the stairs to the main door. "Don't forget to send me that thing you said you'd send."

"I won't."

"I'll call you later."

"Okay."

He pulled open the door and walked out. He kept his head down as he moved to the waiting car, clearly not wanting to be recognized by any early morning joggers. He slipped inside, and I wondered if he looked back. With the tinted windows, I'd never know.

One thing I did know for sure…I was setting myself up for the biggest heartbreak in history.

Kozart

What the fuck had I done? I left ties behind. I *never* left ties behind. It was my number one rule. Always be the one leaving. Aubrey had hit the nail on the head when she called me out on that one.

I should've known after the wedding when I called her, I was digging my own grave. I should've known when I showed up at the bar, I was digging it deeper. But I'd felt like the universe was trying to tell me something. Why, out of all the girls I'd met, did this one have to be able to give me something no one else had?

It had to mean something.

And I would've been a complete idiot if I didn't try to figure it out.

I dropped my head back on the head rest and closed my eyes. I wasn't even tired. I'd slept like I always did after being with Aubrey, like a mother-fucking rock. I just needed to be sure I had my head screwed on straight. Needed to be sure it wasn't screwing with my mojo.

I know I made her no promises, but I couldn't miss the hurt in her eyes when I assured her I was too weak not to fuck groupies. And her hurt—and disappointment in me—sucked.

My phone pinged. I expected it to be my tour manager, pissed that I wasn't in Alabama yet. But it was a text from Aubrey.

I made this for you. I hope you enjoy.

A link sat beneath her words. I clicked on it and found a playlist. A *country* playlist. I laughed to myself as I caught the name of the first song. "Sleep Without You" by Brett Young. Of course, the little smartass would include that first.

I clicked the song and listened to the lyrics. Songwriters heard songs differently than the average listener. We heard things the normal ear didn't catch. And while this song was catchy and I could see why she liked it, it wasn't one I'd be covering in any of my upcoming shows. My fans wanted grit. They wanted angst. They wanted to be taken through the ringer of emotions when they heard me sing.

I understood now why Aubrey enjoyed country. It wasn't angsty. And it gave her hope.

The song ended and another began. The bass in the intro reverberated throughout the car. I checked the title. "Country Girl Shake it for Me," by Luke Bryan. I laughed to myself as he began to sing about country girls, and I knew I needed to message Aubrey. **Thanks for the playlist, country girl.**

Lol!! You do like it!

Listening to it now.

Amazing, right?

I laughed. **Ummmm.**

Stop!

I smiled down at her text, knowing that besides performing, talking to her was slowly becoming one of my favorite things to do.

I was so fucked.

CHAPTER TWELVE

Aubrey

I sipped my frozen macchiato at a corner table in the campus café. I'd just had my voice disorders class and was taking a break before studying for my philosophy test I had in a few days. And by taking a break, I meant I was working on another playlist for Kozart. I wondered if he liked the one I'd sent him. Sure, he said he listened to it. But did he find himself liking any of the songs more than he wanted to? I had a feeling he'd never admit to it even if he had.

"You better have a good reason for not calling yesterday," Mandy said as she slipped into the seat across from me. "I'm dying over here."

"A little dramatic, don't you think?"

Her hands waved around animatedly as her ponytail bounced. "You're dating a freaking rock star."

"*Shhh.*" I glanced around the café, hoping no one was eavesdropping on our conversation. No one was even looking in our direction. "We're not dating," I whispered.

"I caught the two of you in bed, remember?" she argued, her voice rising.

I glanced around. A few people had perked up at her words. "We're friends," I whispered, hoping she would too. "And you need to keep your voice down."

"Why? If it was me, I'd be shouting it from the center of campus and rubbing it in every girl's face who'd ever done me wrong."

I rolled my eyes. "There's nothing to yell. He made me no promises."

"What does that even mean?"

I shrugged. "We're gonna keep talking and see what happens."

Her eyes narrowed. "That's it?"

"That's it."

She paused for a long time, the wheels in her head clearly turning. "Does he want to see you again?"

"Maybe when he's back in town."

"Or, we could take a road trip to one of his shows," she said.

"We could. They put on a really good concert…if you like rock."

She rolled her eyes. "I like anything that comes out of his mouth."

I shook my head, amused. "You didn't tell anyone about him being at my place, right?"

She shook her head. "Are any of his bandmates single?"

"No idea, but I have seen the girls they attract."

Her brows shot up.

"They have their pick after the shows," I said as the bile inched up the back of my throat.

"Z, too?"

"That's why we're just staying friends. He couldn't promise not to be with other girls."

"But you said you were gonna see what happens," she said, confused.

"Yeah, see if he can keep it in his pants. I'd give him a week."

Her mouth twisted regrettably, as if she just realized the predicament I found myself in…again.

"I can't expect him to stay loyal when the temptation is always there," I said. "Besides, we barely even know each other."

"Looked like you were getting to know each other the other night."

Heat crept up my neck and into my cheeks. His kisses *were* amazing. I just wondered if I'd be on the receiving end of them again.

CHAPTER THIRTEEN

Aubrey

I have a surprise for you.

I stared at Kozart's text as I sat in the back of my philosophy class waiting for the professor to pass out the test.

"Phones away and desks cleared," the professor announced before I could respond to the text.

As the test booklets were distributed, my mind spun wondering what my surprise could be. Had he made me my own playlist? Would he be back in Tennessee?

Once I had my test booklet in front of me, I cleared my mind of the rock star who'd begun to consume all my thoughts. I needed to focus on philosophy and only philosophy.

An hour into the test, I had one question left. *Is a cheater ethically or morally wrong?* I read the question over and over again.

The irony was not lost on me.

I considered Geoffrey. Why had he cheated? To feel good. To satisfy his own needs. Because he didn't love me. Did that taint his morals *or* his ethics? Or did the fact that he would've hidden it from me do that? And what about Kozart? Was he any better because he warned me first?

I wrote. And I wrote. And by the end, I'd convinced myself that I'd penned the next Nobel prize winner. I handed in my test booklet and exited the classroom.

Outside, the sun shone down and I walked to a nearby bench, wanting to enjoy the beautiful afternoon while I returned Kozart's text. I slipped out my phone and responded. **I'm listening.**

Three dots danced on my screen, and my stomach bubbled with excitement. **Are you alone?**

I swallowed down my excitement. **Outside on campus but alone on a bench.**

Bouncing dots. **Do you have earbuds?**

I quickly dug in my bag and pulled out my wireless earbuds. **Yup.**

A video popped up on my screen.

I placed my earbuds in and clicked on the video.

My heart began to race.

Kozart sat in front of the camera he'd propped up on something to record himself. His guitar sat in his lap. He looked into the screen, from what appeared to be a hotel room, and said, "I've taken some liberties with this song. I hope you like it."

I sat transfixed as he began to sing "Sleep Without You," the first song on the playlist I'd sent him. And while Brett Young's original version was fast and playful, Kozart slowed it down, giving the lyrics a somber tone as he strummed away at his guitar. His raspy voice sang about being unable to sleep until someone returned home. It's why I'd sent him the song in the first place. The irony of the lyrics and why he claimed to need me were too good to pass up.

As he continued to sing, I hoped the someone *he* sang about was me.

Maybe I was thinking too much. Maybe he just planned to sing every song I'd sent him.

He sang the last verse and strummed the final notes on his guitar. Without saying a word, he stood, leaned toward the phone, and switched off the video.

I stared at the screen long after the video turned off, unable to put into words how I was feeling after that. He'd learned a song I enjoyed and sang it with that raspy rock flare only he could—for *me*. I wondered how many girls he'd done that for. *Had* he done that for other girls? **Will "Country Girl Shake it for Me" be next?**

His response was immediate. Had he been waiting patiently for my thoughts? **Depends. Do you plan to shake it?**

I laughed. **Never know.**

Ha!

I pulled in a breath knowing if I didn't speak honestly, I might never get another song sung for me like that. **It was beautiful. Thank you.**

The dots didn't bounce. Where'd he go?

My thumbs went to work. **Maybe you could add it to your set list.**

The dots bounced. **Nope. That was for your ears only.**

I smiled, loving that response more than I expected to. **Do you have a show tonight?**

We're in Utah.

Good luck.

Rock gods don't need luck.

I laughed.

CHAPTER FOURTEEN

Aubrey

What are you doing right now? Kozart's text came through as I lay in bed Saturday morning.

We'd spoken and texted every day since he'd left, but my heart still sped up when his name appeared on my phone. I smiled and texted him back. **Just laying here.**

Thinking of me?

Thinking about what I want for breakfast.

Liar.

I laughed.

You up for an adventure?

My brows furrowed as I responded. **I'm always up for an adventure.**

I was hoping you'd say that. Look out your window.

My eyes shot to my window, and I eagerly slipped out of bed. A black car sat parked outside. My pulse sped as I texted him. **R u in there?**

No.

My stomach dropped.

I want you to trust me.

I do trust you. I assured him.

Then get dressed and get in. The driver knows where he's going.

I took a moment to calm my excitement, then hurried into the shower. I washed my hair, shaved all the important areas, used lavender body wash, and rinsed in record time. I dried off, got dressed in jeans, a T-shirt, and chucks, then dried my hair. I left my waves a little wild, knowing that's what a real rock chick would do.

Since Eliza's door was closed, I figured she was still sleeping, so I walked to the front door and headed out. Once I reached the car, Kozart's driver got out, opened the back door, and greeted me. I slipped inside. "Get comfortable," he said before closing the door.

I glanced around the empty backseat. Disappointment tugged at my heart. I'd hoped Kozart *was* inside.

Once the driver got back behind the wheel, he switched on country music and I smiled. Had Kozart asked him to do that? I would've assumed he would've bribed him to torture me with rock.

I slipped out my phone and texted Kozart. **Your driver has good taste in country music.**

His text came quickly. **He's fired.**

I laughed and caught the driver glancing at me through the rearview mirror. I looked back down at my phone and sent off another text. **Tell me where I'm going.**

No.

Why?

Patience is a virtue. Text me after your first stop.

How many stops will there be?

I guess you'll just have to wait and see.

Where are you?

My text went unanswered. Damn him.

I sent off a text to Eliza to let her know I'd be gone for a while. Wouldn't want her worrying about me. Then I closed my eyes.

An hour passed before the driver pulled into a fast food restaurant drive-thru and ordered. He pulled forward and grabbed the bag from the worker, handing it back to me. "Here you go."

"Thanks," I said as I reached into the bag and pulled out a burger and soda. I unwrapped the burger to find a double cheeseburger with mustard. I laughed to myself before taking a bite and then texting Kozart. **A burger, huh? I would've ordered a salad.**

His text came quickly. **Not on my watch.**

But you're not here.

I waited for his response as we pulled out of the parking lot. We hadn't left Tennessee, but I noticed we were heading west, toward Nashville.

Another hour or so passed and Kozart still hadn't responded to my last text. Where was he?

The car pulled into downtown Nashville, amidst the hub of tourist activity. Famous bars and restaurants belonging to country music's biggest artists lined the road. People eager to get inside stood on the sidewalks. But my driver didn't stop at any of the hot spots. He did, however, pull to a stop in front of a shop with cowboy boots filling the display window.

He stepped out and circled around to my door, before pulling it open. "Pat will help you inside."

My brows dipped as I stepped out and made my way to the door. I stopped and spun around. "What's your name?"

"Arthur," he said with a small smile.

"Thank you, Arthur." I pushed open the door to the shop and inhaled the smell of leather as I stepped inside. I glanced around. Tourists of all ages picked up boots from the aisles filled with them. Some tried them on and some just browsed the shelves.

"Can I help you?" an older female with a thick Southern drawl asked.

"I'm looking for Pat."

She smiled. "Looks like you found her. You must be Aubrey."

I nodded.

"Well, follow me." She turned and led me to the back of the store where men and women sat trying on boots. "Have a seat. I'd like you to try on some of the boots I pick out and tell me which you like."

"Okay," I said skeptically as I watched her pull boots off the shelves.

She glanced to me. "Size seven, right?"

I nodded. She was good.

It took her no more than a few minutes before she carried an armful of colorful boots to me. "Any of these catch your eye?"

"They're all beautiful. I've never had a pair."

She grinned. "Then let me welcome you to the world of Southern comfort."

I laughed as I took off my chucks and slipped on the first boot she handed me. It was brown with lighter swirls up the sides. I stood, but it felt a little tight in the width.

"Too narrow?" she asked.

I nodded as I sat and slipped it off, grabbing the fire-engine red boot she held out to me. I slipped my foot in and stood. I checked it out in the mirror across from me but didn't love the shine off it. "I think I'll try that one," I said, pointing to a light gray boot with glitter inlay.

"Oh, good choice," Pat said as I sat and pulled off the red boot. She handed me the gray one.

I slipped it on and I didn't even need to stand to know the boot was a perfect fit. It felt like butter on my foot. I could only imagine how much more comfortable it'd be once I'd broken it in.

"Looks good," Pat said.

"It feels good."

She hurried off and grabbed the matching boot. Once I'd slipped that one on and stood, I was convinced. "I'm gonna wear them out," I said, grabbing my chucks.

"Enjoy," she said with a satisfied smile.

"Where's the register?"

"Oh, Hun. They've already been paid for."

My mouth opened slightly. "Thank you, Pat."

"Don't thank *me*. Thank whoever paid."

I hoped I'd get the chance to.

I left the store and was greeted by Arthur standing by the open car door. "Nice boots," he said.

I clicked the heels together. "Thanks, Arthur." I slipped inside the car and pulled out my phone, snapping a picture of my boots and sending it to Kozart. **I love my boots. Thank you!**

I waited for his response, but it didn't come.

Arthur drove for no more than a half mile, pulling down a side road. Tourists passed right by this road, as if they didn't even see it. Arthur pulled to a stop in front of a small nondescript brick building. Unless you squinted, you wouldn't even notice the small sign on the door indicating it was a bar.

Arthur opened my door. "Next stop."

I stepped out and walked to the door, my new boots sparkling in the afternoon sun. The bar door was tinted, which made it impossible to see inside. I tugged on the handle. It was locked. I looked over my shoulder at Arthur.

"Knock," he urged.

I knocked on the door and it swung open. A big man in a tight white T-shirt stood there.

"Hi. I think I'm supposed to be here," I said, having no clue what I'd find inside.

"Name?"

"Aubrey Prescott."

He grabbed a tablet, checking it for my name. His eyes met mine. "You can head back. Just no cell phones in there."

I stepped inside, finding myself smack dab in the middle of a deserted bar. Where the hell was *there*? I glanced back to the man at the door. "Where?"

He motioned toward the back of the room. "Through that door."

"Got it. Thanks." I walked across the empty room, my boots clacking on the hardwood floors. As I stepped through the doorway, I realized a club was in the back. Fifty to seventy-five people stood in front of a small stage watching a man seated with a guitar in his lap and a mic in front of him singing an acoustic version of— *Holy shit!*

I stood frozen to my spot, realizing who the country singer was singing "Sleep Without You." I glanced around, noticing television cameras in all corners of the room, and one right up in front with the fans. I assumed they were filming an all-access show I'd seen on country music television.

He sounded amazing and before I knew it, he was saying goodbye and another artist I knew came on stage and sang two of his biggest hits. One after another, country artists took the stage. I wished my friends were there with me. I wished *Kozart* was there with me.

I slipped out my phone covertly, knowing I wasn't supposed to have it out, and texted him. **OMG!**

He didn't respond. I wondered if my response was enough.

He'd arranged an amazing day for me. One I wouldn't have had if I'd never met him. Was this what life would be like as his girlfriend? Would he spoil me with crazy surprises all the time since he'd rarely be around? I wished he realized spending time with him would be just as good.

Two hours later, I'd seen more artists than I could count singing their best songs acoustically for a select group. We were told the television special would air next month, and I couldn't wait to see it.

Hopefully, Kozart would be there to watch it with me.

CHAPTER FIFTEEN

Aubrey

After the performances, we were ushered out through the still empty bar to the exit. Darkness cloaked the road. Only a few lights from nearby buildings lit the sidewalk. Arthur stood a few yards away by the side of the car. I headed toward him with a big smile, still floating on cloud nine.

"Have a nice time?" he asked.

"An *amazing* time. Did you know where I was going?"

He pulled open the door for me. "Only the address."

I smiled as I slipped inside the backseat, settling in and readying myself for a long trip back to campus.

As Arthur started the engine and headed onto the main road, I pulled out my phone, texting Kozart. **Thank you for an amazing day.**

My text went unanswered like the previous two. Did he have a show tonight? I pulled up his schedule on my phone. He had a show in Vegas last night. My guess was he was hanging there until his show in California on Monday.

I texted the triplets. We went back and forth for a long time which consisted mostly of them telling me how insanely jealous they were that I'd gotten to go to such a killer show and they hadn't. I knew they were teasing me. I knew they were happy for me.

A short while later, the car took a sharp left. My eyes shifted out the window. We weren't on the highway. We weren't anywhere near a highway. We were driving up a long driveway with woods on either side of us. The car eventually stopped, and the engine switched off.

I ducked my head to see out the front window. A huge house, I could only describe as a modernized log cabin, sat high on a hill with floor to ceiling windows overlooking the surrounding forest.

My car door opened, startling me. "You ready?" Arthur asked.

"I'm not sure."

He laughed as he helped me out of the car onto the steep driveway. Once I got my footing, he lifted his chin toward the door beside the three-car garage. A light shone inside. "You can enter through there."

"Thank you, Arthur."

"My pleasure."

I walked to the door, wondering what surprise lay inside. I lifted my hand to knock.

"Just go in," Arthur called.

I twisted the ornate door handle and pushed open the door.

I stepped inside a gorgeous kitchen, with white cabinets, stainless steel appliances, and gray granite countertops. There was a giant island with four drop lights hanging above it. "Hello?" I called, my voice echoing through the cavernous home.

I listened for a response or movement, but heard nothing.

I continued through the kitchen into a dining room. The glass-topped table accentuated with massive leather chairs sat in the center of the room. It was the type of room you knew would be the spotlight of most homes, but got very little use in this home.

I continued my exploration, looking for signs of occupants. I came upon a living area with black leather sofas, a flat-screen the size of a movie screen, and a gorgeous white marble fireplace between two white bookshelves built into the wall.

That's when I saw them.

Amongst the books and art pieces, sat three gold music awards.

I moved toward them.

"Beautiful," a deep voice said behind me.

My pulse picked up speed but I didn't turn. "The awards?"

"You in my house."

I twisted around.

Kozart stood there barefoot in jeans and nothing else.

My body quivered, goosebumps erupting everywhere at the sight of him. "Hi."

He lifted a brow. "Hi?"

Shit. "Thank you."

He smirked and took a step closer to me.

"Thank you for everything," I continued, not wanting to sound ungrateful.

He took another step.

"Everything today has been amazing," I added.

He took another step until he stood right in front of me, his nearness doing crazy things to my belly. "Stop thanking me."

"But—"

He cupped my cheek with his hand and I was done, leaning into it as if starved for his touch. "I wish I could've gone with you."

"You don't like country music."

"But I like you."

A delicious shiver racked through me.

"And I would've given anything to see your face when you realized what you were there to see."

"There will be other things we can do together."

"Oh, there are a lot of things I want to do with you right now."

A tsunami-sized wave gushed through my belly.

He lifted his other hand to cup my other cheek. "Texting isn't cutting it for me."

I pulled in a breath.

"I need to touch you."

Goosebumps rushed up my arms.

"Can I do that, Aubrey? Can I touch you tonight?"

"You're touching me right now."

"In other places."

I swallowed down the lump that shot to my throat and nodded, hypnotized by his blue irises and the rough timber of his voice.

His mouth inched toward mine. When he was a mere breath apart, he whispered, "Ready?"

Tremors rocked through me as his lips touched mine. His tongue dipped inside my mouth, sliding against mine slow and steady. He was in no rush at all.

My hands slipped around his back as his fingers shifted from my cheeks and tunneled through my hair. I groaned as my body arched into him. He kissed me deeper, but still slow and calculated. He eventually pulled away, leaving both of our chests heaving. "I didn't realize how much I missed you until I saw you standing in my house," he said.

"I guess you need to invite me over more often."

He chuckled as his eyes dropped to my feet. "Those boots look good on you."

I laughed at the sparkly boots on my feet, moving them to give him a better view.

"Are you gonna stay with me tonight?" he asked.

"Have you been sleeping?"

He nodded.

"That's a good thing," I said.

"It is, but it makes being away from you harder."

That pile of goo on the floor. That was me.

"So, are you gonna stay?"

"Yes, I'll stay."

A slow smile spread across his face. "Can I show you my room?"

"You don't waste any time."

He laughed as he took my hand and led me up the staircase.

"Your home is beautiful."

"Thanks. I designed it."

"Wow. That's impressive."

He moved us down the long second-floor hallway.

"I'm surprised pictures of you aren't filling every wall."

"God, no. Why would I wanna look at myself?"

"I thought that's what famous musicians do."

"Where do you get your information? I have platinum records framed in my office, but no pictures of me." He pushed open the double doors at the end of the hallway. The white carpet felt like a cloud beneath my feet as I stepped inside a sitting area equipped with a sofa and fireplace. No curtains or blinds covered his floor-to-ceiling windows.

I walked over to them and looked out into the darkness. "There's a lake?"

"Yeah. It's beautiful during the day."

"I bet."

He walked behind me and slipped his arms around my stomach, pressing his chest to my back as he lowered his chin to my shoulder.

"Why are you hidden all the way out here?" I asked.

He was silent for a long time. Had I asked another question he felt uncomfortable answering? Was I being too nosy? "I need the quiet to stay quiet."

My chest constricted, knowing his words carried multiple meanings.

"Out here, I'm truly alone, and I can just shut everything else out."

I closed my eyes, knowing he saw more than a child should have. "I'm sorry."

"Don't be. I'm kind of a loner by nature. So being out here is a good thing for me."

"For a rock star you're kind of boring," I teased. "What about the parties? Girls? Alcohol? You better hope I don't go talking to the tabloids about the boring life you live."

He spun me around unexpectedly and pressed my back to the cool window, caging me in with his arms. "That."

"What?"

"Your sarcasm. That's what makes me sleep."

My brows scrunched together. "You like my sarcasm?"

"I *love* your sarcasm. And I love that I know where I stand with you."

"You *think* you know," I countered.

"I *know* I know," he assured me.

"And where do I stand with *you*?" I asked.

"Well, right now, I'm liking having you pinned between me and this window."

I cocked my head, waiting for an honest answer.

"I haven't touched another girl since we've been talking. It makes me think it might not be so hard after all."

"I'm not congratulating you for keeping it in your pants," I assured him.

"Not looking for it. I just want you to know where you stand. I'm thinking pretty high in my thoughts if I don't want to mess it up."

I stifled a grin. "That's a start."

"That's a fucking *amazing* start," he said. "But I've gotta tell you, porn is not doing the trick. I need you in my bed."

I swallowed down hard. He had to have seen it.

He dropped his forehead to mine. "We do *not* have to do anything you're not comfortable with."

"It's not about comfort, Kozart. It's the knowledge that I could sleep with you tonight, and you could be with someone else tomorrow. You've made me no promises and I'm not trying to force you to. But I like you. I like how I feel when I'm with you and when I talk to you. But we both know I got screwed over. I can't feel that way again. Not with you."

He nodded.

"You've been up front and honest with me. And I respect that. But I have to respect myself in the morning too."

His lips twisted. "I got it."

"Good. Now show me the rest of this ginormous room."

He smiled as he pulled me away from the window and moved us through a doorway between the sitting area and his actual bedroom.

A king-sized bed was the centerpiece of his room. A black down comforter covered the bed and a mountain of black-and-white cow print throw pillows were piled against the black headboard.

"Now *this* looks like a rock star's bedroom."

He gave me a sidelong glance. "Why?"

"Black orgy-sized bed."

"Of course, you'd say that," he said.

"Am I wrong?"

"You're the only girl I've ever had in here."

I choked on my laughter. "Yeah, right."

"I'm serious. I don't take anyone here."

"Why not?"

He shrugged. "It's mine. And I don't have to share it unless I want to."

My heart splintered. He'd never had *anything* of his own. This was his, and no one could take it away from him. "Thanks for sharing it with me."

He said nothing.

I took in the rest of the room. A framed photo of him and his bandmates was on his black dresser. I walked over and picked it up. They all looked a lot younger.

"That's right after we signed our contract," he explained. "It was my birthday."

I placed the photo down and turned to him. "When's your birthday?"

"October fifteenth."

I made a mental note, knowing I'd want to get him something.

"There's a bathroom over there," he said, pointing to a door on the far wall. "I got you some clothes for tonight and tomorrow."

I raised a brow. "A little presumptuous."

"I hoped. I never presumed."

"Right." I rolled my eyes, and his chuckle followed me as I walked inside the bathroom. I closed the door and sat on the edge of the six-person Jacuzzi tub. There was a gorgeous glass shower with multiple shower heads and a flat-screen television built into the wall tiles.

A pile of folded clothes with a new toothbrush and toothpaste sat waiting for me on the marble-topped vanity. I slipped off my new boots, jeans, and top and washed my face in the sink. I brushed my teeth and then searched for pajamas in the pile of brand-new jeans, shirts, and bras and panties he'd left for me.

I picked up an oversized black T-shirt that I assumed belonged to Kozart. He'd clearly picked it out as my pajamas. *Guys.* I slipped off my bra and tugged the shirt over my head, piling my own clothes on the vanity. I pulled a hair band off my wrist and tied my hair into a messy knot on the top of my head. I checked myself in the mirror one last time before stepping out of the bathroom.

Kozart wasn't in bed. He wasn't in the bedroom at all.

I found him on the sitting area sofa with his legs on top of the leather ottoman. He'd turned on the fireplace and stared into it.

"Thanks for the clothes," I said, making my way over to him.

With a cocky grin, his eyes drifted up my bare legs. "What can I say? The vision of you in my T-shirt has carried me through some lonely nights."

Amused, I shook my head and sat down beside him, tucking my knees beneath me and nestling into him.

He wrapped his arm around me and pulled me closer. The warmth of the fire and Kozart's soapy scent soothed me as we watched the dancing flames. They were beautiful, quite like a melody, swaying and crackling to their own beat.

"This is nice," I said.

"What?"

"Sitting here with you. Doing normal stuff."

He leaned down and pressed a kiss to my head. "I need normal in my life."

We both fell silent watching the fire for a long time.

"How'd you get me into that taping?" I asked.

"I share a record label with some of those guys. Go figure."

"See? You're so wrapped up in *rock* music you don't realize there's a whole other genre out there."

"Oh, I realize all right."

"Are you leaving in the morning for California?"

"How'd you know my next show's in California?"

"I might've checked when you weren't returning my texts earlier. I thought maybe you were in the middle of a concert."

"Nope. Got the day off today and tomorrow. What shall we do?"

I sighed, totally doing a happy dance in my mind. "Swim."

"Swim?"

"You have your own lake, don't you?"

He chuckled. "I don't actually own the lake."

"Either way, we can swim in it, right?"

"It's getting cold, but yeah."

"Yeah?"

"If you're getting in, hell yeah." He stood from the sofa and held out his hand, pulling me up and leading me into his room.

"What side do you sleep on?" I asked.

"The middle."

I pulled back the comforter on the right side and crawled under. "Then you won't mind if I take this side."

His gaze heated as he stared at me in his bed. "Not at all." He unsnapped his jeans and pushed them down his legs, kicking them off his feet. "I love having you in my bed."

"Most guys do."

His eyes darkened. "They better not if they know what's good for them."

I rolled my eyes. "Retract the claws, big bad rock star."

He smirked as he climbed under the covers in his boxers and turned me on my side away from him. He wrapped his arms around me, pulling my back flush against his chest.

We lay in silence, though my mind whirled with uncertainty. Why wasn't he trying to kiss me? He was the one who asked if he could touch me tonight. Had he changed his mind? Had he realized he wasn't really into me that way now that we were in the same place?

One thing *was* for sure. Being in bed with Kozart, with his arms holding me tightly, was difficult given the range of emotions I was feeling. And *I* was the one who'd told him I couldn't sleep with him. The soft sound of his breathing was something I couldn't seem to get enough as it drifted over my ear and shoulder. I wanted to hear it every night and that thought alarmed the hell out of me.

"Aubrey?"

"Yes?"

"I wanna make you feel good."

A lump shot to my throat. I swallowed it down.

"Will you let me?" His lips dropped to the area beneath my ear and without waiting for my response, he peppered my skin with open-mouthed kisses.

My eyes rolled into the back of my head as he kissed his way to the nape of my neck, dragging his tongue up the hollow space as his hands slid down to my bare thighs.

Tingles shot to my core.

"Tell me if you want me to stop," he said against my skin.

When I said nothing, his hands trailed up my hips. He reached the hem of my T-shirt and paused for a minute, giving me time to stop him. I didn't. His hands slipped under my T-shirt and coasted slowly up my stomach, his smooth fingers leaving tremors in their wake.

I held my breath as his hands skated up and over my breasts. My head dropped back as his mouth moved to the crook of my neck. His thumbs and forefingers tugged on my nipples as he sucked on my neck, taunting me with the knowledge of what his mouth would feel like elsewhere.

I pulled in a sharp breath.

"Do you like that?" he asked, sucking and tugging simultaneously again.

Zingers shot between my thighs.

"Oh, you do, don't you?" he taunted, doing it again and again.

Gahhhhh.

Throbbing began between my legs—deep, bass drum, throbbing.

Kozart's hands left my breasts and drifted down my stomach, leaving me yearning for more.

I released a huff of disappointment.

"Don't worry," he whispered. "You're gonna enjoy this more." His hands reached my panties and his fingers slipped underneath the material.

"You might want to hold your breath," he teased as his middle finger slipped over my folds. "Ah, nice and wet."

I groaned deep in my throat.

"See? I told you I could make you feel good." His finger plunged inside me, moving in and out slowly. As my breathing sped up, he added another finger, pumping both in and out. As if the sensation wasn't enough, he pressed his thumb to my clit. I didn't know which sensation to focus on. They both pulsed in their own magical way, making it nearly impossible to keep my sanity.

His mouth moved to my ear and he nibbled his way around it, biting gently.

"Kozart," I whispered, nearly breathless.

"Yeah, babe?"

"Please don't stop."

There was a smile in his voice. "No chance I'm stopping when I need to hear how you sound coming on my fingers."

I swallowed down my arousal at his dirty words. My breathing became embarrassingly labored as his thrusts became deeper, his thumb somehow still circling.

"Fuck this," he said as he withdrew his fingers and moved away from me.

"What?"

He pushed me onto my back and climbed on top of me. He wasn't lying about liking me in his shirt. He hadn't even tried to remove it. He moved slowly down my body, his nose running between my breasts and over my stomach until he reached my panties. He tucked his pinkies into the sides and pulled them down my legs.

My chest rose and fell with each heavy breath as he spread my legs at the knees and buried his face between my thighs.

I gasped as his mouth closed over my clit and he sucked it. Hard.

Holy mother of God.

My writhing body and quiet whimpers revealed my arousal.

He took that as his cue, lapping away at it, over and over again. He knew I was close, so he swiped his tongue along my folds in a slow torturous path from back to front, circling my clit at the end. Again and again.

My legs began to quiver as something inside me coiled tightly. "Oh, *Goddddd.*" My body unraveled, tremors rocking through me and coursing out to every nerve ending. My body trembled, quaking as he milked me for everything he could. My knees closed around his head. The sensations were too great and I needed him to stop. But he persisted for a little longer then relented, lifting his head from between my thighs. Only then did I release him, my legs dropping shamelessly open.

I lay there, basking in the aftereffects of what he'd done. Geoffrey had *never* made me feel like that. *Never.*

Kozart crawled back over me, covering me with his body.

I didn't move, just opened my eyes to find his satisfied smirk. "That was so good."

He chuckled as he lightly brushed my loose strands of hair off my face. "I can do it all night long."

"Promise?"

He leaned down and kissed me. The taste of me on his tongue didn't even faze me. Probably because I was wiped out and on the cusp of the most amazing sleep I'd ever had.

CHAPTER SIXTEEN

Aubrey

My eyes popped open. Kozart's room was aglow with sunshine and my clit was throbbing like—*holy shit.*

My head shot up and my eyes cast down.

Kozart lay between my legs, his face buried between my thighs.

"Oh my God," I moaned, a mixture of surprise and pleasure.

He looked up with a conspiratorial grin.

"You don't have to do that."

"Oh, I know I don't have to. I *want* to," he assured me. "I almost couldn't sleep last night thinking about doing it again." He blew on my folds sending my head back into the pillow and my eyes clenching. His mouth continued its assault, his tongue lapping away at my clit.

It took no more than a few minutes and my breathing became labored, cutting through the otherwise silent room. "Oh, *God.*" My eyes pinched tightly as the coiling built. I didn't want it to end, but my body betrayed me. The coil released. My body trembled, my skin hummed, and my knees locked around Kozart's head to stop his glorious torture. But like the previous night, he didn't stop. "*Please,*" I begged, the sensations too powerful.

Finally, he relented, lifting his head and climbing on top of my limp body.

"I could so get used to being woken up that way," I said, all sleepy and content.

"Well, I'm up for the job."

"If only you weren't gone most of the year."

"There is that," he said.

I looked him right in the eyes. "Thank you. I know I'm not making things easy."

His brows scrunched. "Are you crazy? I enjoy pleasuring you."

I scrunched my nose. "Did you really just say 'pleasuring you'?"

His lips kicked up in the corners. "I did."

I laughed.

"Why are you laughing?"

"You know why I'm laughing."

"Okay. So maybe I sounded like a sleazy guy from a '70s porno, but you knew what I meant."

We lay like that for a long time, my body following the movements of his breathing as we enjoyed the silence. Enjoyed each other.

"*Is* this enough for you?" I asked, the thought slowly weighing on my mind.

"Time spent with you is enough. I thought you understood that when I told you it's why I sleep."

"But—"

"But nothing. Let me decide. Okay? Stop trying to convince me I need something else."

I said nothing, his exasperation taking me by surprise.

"I'm sorry," he said. "It's just…I'm happy right now. Let me just be happy instead of telling me why I shouldn't be."

I nodded into his chest, realizing it's what I'd been doing. I'd been trying to sabotage this thing from the start because I didn't want to be hurt. I didn't want *him* to hurt me.

He rolled off of me and sat on the edge of the bed, his fingers tunneling through his tussled hair as his eagle tattoo stared at me.

I rolled onto my side and waited for him to say something, scared I'd pushed him too far. Pushed him away.

"I'm gonna head downstairs to start breakfast," he said as he stood.

"You cook?"

"Survival of the fittest. You learn what you need to do to get by."

I nodded, knowing why he'd needed to learn to be self-sufficient. I wondered how many people knew about his childhood. Wondered if he confided this easily in others.

As soon as he left the room and I heard his feet padding down the stairs, I fell onto my back. I needed to get a grip. I needed to give this thing between us a real chance. I needed to trust him that he wouldn't purposely hurt me. He was a rock star for Christ's sake. And I was clearly hoping he'd remain a monk for me.

Was I being fair?

Was I holding off sleeping with him because I needed him to prove himself to me?

Hadn't he proven himself to me already? I was in his bed, the one he swore he'd never shared with anyone else. We spoke daily. He recorded a song for me. He'd sent me on an amazing adventure tailor-made for me.

What the hell was I waiting for?

After brushing my teeth, freshening up, and pulling my hair out of the knot, I joined him downstairs still wearing only his T-shirt and a new pair of panties. He'd prepared veggie omelets for both of us. "Wow, looks good."

He swung around from his spot at the sink with a smirk. "Me or the food?"

I laughed, and just like that I knew I was forgiven for what happened upstairs. I slipped onto one of the stools at his island and checked him out in his boxers. "The food of course."

"Liar."

He carried over a cup of coffee and placed it beside my omelet. "I wasn't sure how you liked it so I put out cream and sugar."

"Thank you," I said, spooning lots of sugar into my black coffee.

"You want coffee with your sugar?" he asked, slipping onto the stool beside me.

I smiled. "I like things sweet."

"I'll have to remember that."

I dug into my omelet, savoring the taste. "This is good," I said once I finished chewing.

"When are you gonna learn I do everything good?"

I rolled my eyes. "Your ego knows no bounds."

He chuckled.

"You don't like coffee?" I asked, noticing his tall glass of ice water.

"I don't like anything that keeps me up at night."

I nodded, understanding his need to avoid caffeine.

Once we finished breakfast, I loaded our dishes and glasses into the dishwasher while Kozart cleaned the pan and spatula in the sink.

"Are you a fast runner?" Kozart asked as he wiped his hands with a dish towel.

I turned to look at him with inverted brows. "I guess."

He tossed the towel onto the counter and then moved to the side door. "Race you to the lake?"

My eyes widened. "Now?"

He threw open the door and spun outside. "Now."

I followed him as he jogged behind his house and over the expansive green grass.

"I'm letting you lead," I called to him, only a few feet behind.

His laughter carried into the woods as he disappeared within the trees. I kept pace with him. Not only was I not going to lose the race, but I didn't know the path to the lake. That's when I stepped onto a perfectly landscaped walking path that twisted us downhill through the woods. I was on his heels. He knew it, too. I laughed as I passed him, stopping on the dock that stretched into the water at the end of the path.

"I let you win," Kozart assured me as his arm came around my waist.

I smiled, awaiting his embrace, but instead, he lifted me off my feet and jumped into the water with me in his arms.

I screamed before we both plunged under water. The lake was cold. Damn cold. He released me under water and we both came up to the surface, our heads bouncing like buoys as we kicked our legs beneath us to stay afloat. "It's freezing!"

He laughed. "I warned you."

I dropped my head back, pushing my hair out of my face. "But it feels good."

"You think?"

"It's refreshing."

"My manhood is shriveling to nothing."

I burst out laughing. "Thanks for taking me in with you. I probably would've wimped out once I felt how cold it was."

He waded closer to me. "I doubt that. You seem like someone who takes on a challenge head first."

"Like the race I just won?"

"I let you win."

I smirked. "Liar."

With our faces now a few inches apart, Kozart leaned forward and pressed his cold lips to mine. Right when I thought things were about to heat up in the cold water, he grasped my shoulders and dunked me under.

I held my breath as I went under, resurfacing quickly and laughing as I did. "Real nice."

Kozart's laughter mixed with mine. I loved how carefree he was when it was just us. I wondered, since he had to be so mature all the time being the leader of a band and always under a microscope, if time spent with me gave him the chance to be a kid again—the kid he never really got to be.

I flipped myself backward, doing a backflip underwater before resurfacing again.

"Was that a backflip?" he asked, wading closer.

"It was." I backed away playfully, to avoid being dunked again. "I'm full of surprises."

"Yes, you are," he said, his eyes smoldering in a way that dipped my belly.

"I used to be a gymnast," I explained, trying to keep myself afloat while *not* focusing on that look in his eyes for too long.

"Oh yeah?"

"Then I broke my leg, and I just couldn't compete at the same level."

"That sucks."

"Yeah, but my grandparents spent a lot of time with me while I was recovering. My grandpa had just had a stroke and his speech was affected. I used to sit with him for hours trying to help him pronounce his words correctly."

"That's why you want to be a speech pathologist?"

I nodded. "That and I hear stories about kids like you who stuttered and didn't know there were techniques out there to assist you, and I want to be able to help them too."

He stared at me, his eyes heating my cold body. Did he know he had the ability to do that with a single gaze? "That's awesome, Aubrey."

"Were kids mean to you because of your stutter?"

"Brutal."

"I hate each and every one of those little assholes."

He chuckled. "Don't worry. I didn't let it hurt me too much."

Too much? *Grrr*. My heart ached for that little kid he once was. "Well, look at you now," I said. "Eat your hearts out little assholes."

The sound of his laughter echoed around us.

We waded in the water for a couple more minutes. "You ready?" he asked.

I nodded.

The walk back to his house was a cold one. But once we reached the backyard, he ducked into the garage and grabbed us two towels. He wrapped one around me and pulled me into him. Wrapping the other around the both of us.

I tipped my head back to catch his eyes. "Much better."

"You know what will feel even better?" he asked.

I shook my head.

"A hot shower."

"Mmmm," I murmured, the thought already warming me.

"And a fire."

"Sold."

We walked inside and upstairs to his room. "I'll give you some privacy. You can shower in here. I'll shower in one of the guest rooms."

"It's okay. I don't mind waiting for you to be done."

His head retracted. "You sure?"

I nodded.

He leaned in and kissed me. "I'll be fast." He disappeared into the bathroom, and as soon as I heard the shower switch on, I sat on the edge of his bed.

The sight of him in the kitchen. The playfulness of our race. The silliness of him pulling me into the lake. It was all...perfect.

I stared at the closed bathroom door, visualizing him in the shower, all naked and wet.

Did I have the nerve?

Could I be brave and bold and all the things I liked to believe I was?

I stood from the bed and padded my way to the closed bathroom door. The shower was still on. The vision of him in there urged me on. I tapped on the door.

"Yeah?"

"Can I come in?"

There was silence on his end for a minute before he answered me. "Sure."

I pulled open the bathroom door and steam billowed out. The glass shower door was fogged, but I could still discern the outline of Kozart's naked body which sent goosebumps dancing across my skin. I moved to the sink and brushed my teeth.

Don't back down now, Aubrey.

I finished brushing then turned toward the shower, dropping the towel to the floor and tugging off my wet T-shirt and panties. I moved to the shower door and pulled it open.

The surprise in Kozart's eyes caused me a second of panic. But his look quickly morphed to desire.

My eyes lowered down to his soap-covered chest and finely chiseled body. *Whoa boy.* My eyes shot up to his cocky grin as he stepped back in the shower, giving me room to enter.

I stepped in. The multi-headed shower sprayed water from several different directions.

Kozart stayed against the wall, watching me contemplate my next move. I stepped to him. My hands pressed against his chest as water soaked me from two different directions, the warm water instantly heating my chilled body. Kozart moved my wet hair away from my face, a gentle move that showed me he didn't want to push me to do anything I didn't want to do.

"I want to touch you," I said, mesmerized by my hand drifting over his smooth chest.

"Touch away," he said, a smile in his voice.

My hands drifted down slowly, over every perfect inch. My thumbs spread, moving over the glorious V carved into his hips.

"You definitely *are* full of surprises," he said.

My hands continued down. It was now-or-never time. I grasped hold of him in one hand, making a fist. He hissed through his teeth as I moved my hand slowly up and down his hardening erection.

"You have no idea how good that feels," he said, his head dropping back against the tiles and his eyes pinching shut.

I continued pumping my fist. Kozart's ragged breaths urged me on. I considered dropping to my knees, but also considered how many girls must've done it before me. I wasn't one of his groupies, and I wouldn't allow myself to be thought of as such. I leaned forward, pressing kisses to his chest as my hand continued moving.

"Aubrey," he moaned. "This is the best kind of torture." His hands cupped my cheeks and he urged my face toward his. His wet lips captured mine, his tongue pushing inside my mouth and tangling in a purposeful race with mine. He wasn't taking it slowly. He was conveying his need for more.

The water mixing with our need for each other was so freaking hot. I arched into him. My wet breasts pushed against his chest as my hand continued moving. He groaned into my mouth and his erection thickened. I wanted him inside me. I wanted him groaning *because* of me. I wanted him hissing my name when he came. But could I do it? Could I let him in?

He pulled back an inch. "God, you're amazing."

His words and the feel of him in my hand was such a heady combination.

"But this is going to be over embarrassingly fast," he admitted as he grasped my wrists, causing me to release him. He lifted my arms above my head in one of his hands. He leaned forward and kissed me, his teeth nipping before his tongue delved inside. I slipped my hands free, and he groaned into my mouth as they slipped around to his lower back.

My fingers coasted down and over his ass. I dug my nails in before drifting my fingertips up and over his back. His solid muscles created deep valleys and ridges all the way up. My hands traveled higher, over his broad shoulders and down to his biceps. My fingertips trailed over them as if memorizing every defined line.

Kozart shifted his hips, his erection slipping against my stomach.

I couldn't stop myself.

I lifted my leg around his hip and he grabbed it behind the knee. He didn't move, letting me stay in charge of how far we took it. I shifted my hips, rubbing against him. Back and forth, up and down, as we kissed.

He pulled away from my mouth and buried his lips in my neck, kissing his way down my collarbone with calculated, opened-mouth kisses. "All you have to do is ask," he breathed.

I said nothing, just kept rubbing shamelessly against his erection. The tip bounced off my clit sending zingers rocking through me. My head dropped to the side, giving his mouth easier access and me a minute to process what the hell I was doing. It would be so easy to let him in. So easy to take it further. So easy to let him make me feel good while doing the same for him.

But why was I contemplating it?

Was I scared of losing him?

Scared of sending him into the bed of a groupie to find satisfaction elsewhere?

He spun us around, pressing my back to the cold tiles.

I giggled, surprised and suddenly chilly.

"You are so fucking hot," he growled, his eyes staring into mine. "But if this is not going *there*, you need to let me get on my knees right now."

My heart ricocheted off the wall of my chest, my breathing labored.

"I don't care either way," he assured me. "But you're coming one way or another."

"I want you," I said.

"But?"

I shook my head. "But nothing."

His eyes widened, as if he didn't expect that response. "And you want to do it in here?"

I nodded. "Unless it's a place…" My voice trailed off, not wanting to think about anyone but us in the moment.

His eyes shot down, unable to deny what he knew I was about to say. "I've never been with *you*. That makes it all different."

I nodded, appreciating his reassurance.

"I'll be right back." He hurried out of the shower and opened a drawer in the bathroom vanity. When he returned, he held a condom.

I watched as he rolled it on away from the spray of the shower heads.

He stepped toward me, walking me against the tile wall again and pressing his forehead to mine. "I don't want to disappoint you."

"No promises," I assured him, though I wished more than anything *this* was the promise.

He wasted no time, dropping his hands to my breasts and dragging his thumbs over my nipples. My head dropped against the tiles as he bent and sucked my left nipple hard.

Gahhhh.

He moved to my other nipple, sucking it just as hard, sending zingers between my thighs.

He lowered one of his hands down my side and over my hip. It drifted across my lower stomach and slid down between my legs. He continued sucking my nipples as his fingers trailed over my folds, his thumb pressing to my clit.

Oh. My. God.

His fingers plunged inside me, pumping in and out, slow and steady.

"*Kozart.*"

"Yeah, babe?"

"I'm ready."

"Oh, I can feel that," he said, but didn't let up.

"Please," I panted.

"Please what?"

"You know what."

"I need to hear you say it," he taunted.

"Fuck me, Kozart."

"Those are some dirty words for a sweet country girl."

He withdrew his fingers and grabbed hold of himself, pumping a few times before running the head over my folds. "This is what your dirty words did to me," he said.

I groaned shamelessly as the head bounced off my clit.

"I don't think I'm gonna be able to be gentle," he said.

"Good."

He twisted me around, pressing my chest against the wet tiles. I braced myself with my hands on the wall as his hands came around and cupped my breasts. His erection pressed to my ass as he leaned into me, pinching my nipples, then soothing the sting with the swipe of his thumbs. He purposely ran the head up and down the slit between my ass as he played with my nipples.

My panting became loud as the pounding in my clit intensified, beating in tandem with my pulse.

"You ready for this?" he asked, pressing his mouth to my ear.

"God, yes."

He abandoned one of my breasts and his hand dropped to his erection. He slipped it between my legs and playfully moved it back and forth, gliding it over my folds.

My head dropped back onto his shoulder, enjoying the feel of him sliding over me.

Finally, he positioned himself at my entrance.

My eyes pinched shut, ready to take all of him in.

He wasted no time, pushing inside me with one hard thrust. Between my arousal and the shower water, I was soaked, making everything easier. He braced his hands over mine on the wall and buried his mouth in my neck, sucking away with sexy opened-mouthed kisses as he thrust inside me. "You feel so good," he groaned.

"Mmmmm."

"Reach down and touch yourself," he hissed.

I slipped a hand free from his and reached down to my throbbing clit. I wanted to do whatever he wanted. I circled my clit with my middle finger. The coiling began, quickly intensifying.

"You are so fucking hot," he said, all gruff and turned on.

His words, mixed with his dick stretching me wide, was almost too much to handle.

His breathing became ragged as his thrusts became harder. He reached down and grabbed my hips, pounding in and out of me. He was close, but I was closer.

"*Kozart.*"

"One more minute," he gritted out as his thrusts became deeper.

My body uncoiled in a rush of euphoria. Quivers spread out to every part of my body as I panted through the most intense orgasm I'd ever had.

Kozart thrust a few more times then stilled inside me, dropping his mouth to my neck and letting out a low feral moan.

My knees threatened to give out. He must've felt it because he pulled out of me then slipped his arms around my stomach. He pulled me onto his lap as he sat on the bench in the corner of the massive shower, away from the spray of water. His arms tightened around me as I rested my head on his shoulder. We sat in silence for a long time as the shower rained down around us.

My body had never felt something like that before. *Ever.*

But what was he thinking?

Had I given it up too quickly?

Did he regret what we'd done?

I wanted to ask. I *really* wanted to ask. But I was terrified to know the answers.

"I guess I know what it feels like now," he said, so quiet it was almost lost in the water raining into puddles on the shower floor.

"What?"

"Making love to someone you care about."

Oh. My. *Freaking.* God.

Kill me now because life could *not* get any better.

He pushed my wet tendrils away from my face. "I just wanna look at you."

"Why?"

"Because I'm memorizing this moment. These feelings. Your face."

He was definitely trying to kill me. I let him look at me. And I looked at him. The curve of his lips. The gaze in his eyes. The feel of his touch. If I wasn't careful, I might begin to feel something deeper than like. Something that could leave me beyond heartbroken.

"Sex in showers," I said.

"What?" he asked.

"I'm adding it to my profile."

"I'm thinking you won't be needing that profile anymore. Unless you wanna see me kick the ass of any guy trying to get near my girl."

"Your girl?"

He leaned over, and when his lips were an inch away from mine, he said, "*My* girl."

My belly rippled as he closed the distance between us and kissed me, slow and gentle. A perfect parallel to his perfect words.

I pulled out of the kiss first. "But just think of all the guys who'll be interested once I make that addition. I'm not sure I'm ready to give all that up."

He picked me up with a roar and carried me out of the shower, through the bathroom, and into his room, tossing me on the bed as he discarded his condom. When he returned, he crawled over my wet naked body and pressed me into his mattress. "What will it take for you to give up those other guys?"

"Did you mean what you said? Or was that just after-sex talk?"

His brows dipped. "After-sex talk?"

I nodded.

"I say what I mean, Aubrey. I thought you understood that. Good or bad, I'll give it to you straight."

I closed the distance between us and kissed him hard, smiling as I pulled away. "Then let me give it to you straight. Go make me a snack."

Laughter burst out of him. "Maybe I want to lay here with you a little while longer."

"Well, maybe my stomach doesn't care."

He smiled down at me for a long time. I wondered what he was thinking. Was he considering what he'd all but assured me by calling me his girl? Was it finally hitting him that he couldn't be with other girls anymore if we began a relationship? Was he having regrets? His smile told me he wasn't thinking any of those things.

I wished I wasn't.

He rolled off me and stood. "I like you naked in my bed," he grinned as he walked to his dresser and pulled on a pair of boxers.

"I like you naked anywhere," I joked.

He laughed. "Meet you downstairs?"

I nodded, falling onto my back when he left the room. This was going to suck if it ended. Because I knew, with much certainty, I was already too far gone.

CHAPTER SEVENTEEN

Aubrey

We spent the remainder of the day curled up on the sofa in front of his fireplace. Kozart in basketball shorts and me in a Savage Beasts T-shirt he gave me. My head lay on his shoulder while his arm kept me tucked perfectly into his side. Most of the time was spent in comfortable silence. I wondered where his thoughts lay, since mine were on the minutes ticking down until I knew I'd have to leave.

"When are you gonna sing me my song?" I asked.

"I already sang you your song."

"Not *to* me."

He said nothing for a long time. "I've never sang a song to anyone before."

"Yeah, right."

"I haven't. I've sung for small crowds, but not a song specifically for someone."

"Would you feel uncomfortable doing it?"

He said nothing, and I wondered if he worried about stuttering in this type of situation.

A few minutes passed and he began humming the beginning of the song into my ear. The vibration sent a delicious shiver skimming down my spine. I thought that's all I was gonna get until he softly began singing the lyrics. Each word meaning so much more than the lyrics other people heard when listening to the song. These sentiments were directed at me. These were Kozart's honest feelings about being unable to sleep without *me*.

"I love my song," I said when he finished singing. "Thank you for singing it."

"I wish you loved *my* songs," he said with a smile in his voice, though I knew he wished I was a rock chick.

"I love that you sing them. I just don't feel them the way I feel when you sing something like you just did to me."

He nodded. "I get it. I just don't like it."

"I'll tell you what. When you put together your next album, let me hear the songs first."

"You wanna be my producer now?"

"No, but you know I'll be honest with you."

He laughed.

"Speaking of honesty…"

I felt his body tense. "I'm listening," he said warily.

"I really don't like double cheeseburgers with mustard."

Laughter burst out of him. "Then why'd you order one?"

"You threatened to throw me out if I got a salad. And I really didn't want you to throw me out."

"Thank you for being honest."

"So, you won't kick me out if I like salads?"

"I will not kick you out if you like salads. Tofu? Yes. Salads, no."

"I hate tofu."

"Good."

* * *

I lay in the backseat with my head on Kozart's lap. The weekend had been unbelievable but now reality was about to slap me in the face. With every town sign we passed, my heart grew heavier. We were getting closer to my place.

"So…" I said.

"You say 'So' every time you have something to say, but don't really want to say it," Kozart said, his fingers playing with my hair.

"You know what *you* do every time you don't want to answer a question? You laugh," I countered.

"Well, I'm glad to see we're both paying attention. Now, what were you gonna say?" he asked.

"I'm not needy. I swear."

"You're the least needy girl I've ever met. I couldn't even get you to call me. Just say what you wanna say."

"What are you doing for Thanksgiving?"

"Thanksgiving?"

"Yeah."

"I have no idea. I'm usually on the road. Why?"

"Well, I was just thinking, if you need somewhere to go, I go home and we have a nice dinner."

"Are you inviting me to meet your parents?"

I cringed. "When you say it like that, it's sounds needy."

He chuckled.

"I just wanted to make sure you weren't alone. I mean, I know you don't have family to spend the day with."

"My band's my family now."

"No, I get that. I just wanted to offer."

He said nothing for a long time. Then he eased me up so I sat up beside him. He gently gripped my chin, turning my face to look at him. "Thank you for inviting me. If I'm around, I would love to spend the day with you and your family."

I said nothing, just nodded.

He leaned closer. "Never feel uncomfortable asking me something. Especially something as thoughtful as that." He pressed his lips to mine and kissed me slow. I wanted to get lost in the kiss. Wanted to remember it because who knew when I'd see him again. But he pulled back, his thumb drifting over my bottom lip.

"Can I ask you something?" I said.

He nodded.

"Are your parents still alive?"

He shrugged. "I have no idea. They chose drugs and crime over me. I'm good with never seeing them again."

"Would it hurt you to hear if they weren't still living?"

"Don't think I'm an asshole for saying this, but no. Not even a little. They threw me to the wolves and never looked back."

I slipped my arms around him and held on. I'm not sure if he needed me to, but I knew I needed to. I wanted to hug the little stuttering boy who was placed in foster care. I wanted him to know he had people—who actually knew him—who cared about him.

Our car pulled to a gradual stop. I lifted my head and dread filled me when I realized we were in front of my condo. "Shit."

"Fuck," he said.

"Dammit," I said with a grin.

The car door opened and Arthur stood there.

"You can get back in the car, Arthur. I'm gonna need a second," Kozart said.

Arthur closed the door and returned to the driver's seat.

I lifted my brows. "You want me all to yourself, huh?"

"More than you know." He pulled me into his lap so I straddled him. He grasped the sides of my head gently. "I told you I couldn't make you any promises before, but I want you to know I'm promising you something now."

I stared into his eyes. They'd never been more serious. My heart walloped, ready to jump out of my chest. I nodded.

He kissed me hard and I knew it was our last for a while. When he pulled away, my fingertips trailed over his cheeks and the stubble on his jawline, memorizing it.

"Come on," he said. "Let me walk you to the door."

I climbed off his lap and opened the door, stepping out first.

He followed me out, his eyes shooting around. The darkness concealed us, but he'd forgotten his hat. I wondered if he felt vulnerable without it. He linked his fingers with mine and walked me to the door. On the front step, he turned to me. "If I come in, I'm gonna have a real hard time leaving. So, I need to leave you here."

I nodded.

He stepped to me, cupping my cheeks and pressing his lips to mine. I knew better than to wrap my arms around him out in the open. He pulled back and took off for the car, his head down. He didn't look back. He never looked back.

I watched until he was inside, then turned to the front door and disappeared inside, hoping *I'd* be able to sleep.

Kozart

My phone pinged as soon as my red eye landed in California. I hoped it was Aubrey checking to see if I'd landed safely. But it was a text from my publicist, Brielle.
Tell me you're NOT fucking some teenager.

My thumbs pounded away at my screen. **What?**

Her next text popped up. **There are pictures of you leaving college housing in Tennessee. Some blurry ones even look like you're kissing her.**

Fuck.

Your fans want a man, Z. They don't want to hear you're fucking underage girls.

I fired back. **I'm not fucking underage girls.**

We both know it doesn't matter. Photos never lie.

I dropped my phone on the seat beside me and let my head fall back. *Fuck. Fuck. Fuck.*

My publicist hated cleaning up after me. Don't get me wrong. She kicked ass at it. But I hated giving her work to do because of me. Treyton was always caught on video leaving strip clubs with strippers, but not me. I usually tried to keep my private shit private.

Even still, I needed to text Aubrey, knowing I had to keep it real with her. **Pictures are floating around of me leaving your place. If anyone asks questions, play dumb.**

She didn't respond. I stared at my phone for the next hour as the car drove me from the airport to the hotel. I was well aware that it was the middle of the night in Tennessee, but I still needed her to respond.

My phone pinged while I slept in the hotel a couple hours later. **Sorry! Was asleep. No worries. Never heard of you.**

I smiled at her words, and slowly my publicist's concerns were a thing of the past.

CHAPTER EIGHTEEN

Aubrey

"He did what?" Eliza shrieked from my bedroom doorway.

"It was amazing," I said, trying not to sound as happy as I actually was.

She fell onto my bed beside me and sighed. "Z freaking Savage is a God."

"You have no idea," I said, before we both broke into laughter.

My phone vibrated on my nightstand. I grabbed it, hoping to see another text from Kozart, but it was from Geoffrey. **I knew he looked familiar.**

I jolted up.

A rock star? Seriously, Aubs?

"What is it?" Eliza asked, sitting up beside me.

"People actually know."

"People know what?" she asked.

"About me and Kozart."

"So, what? You'll be a legend."

"He didn't want me talking to anyone."

"He really is a god," Eliza said.

I bumped her with my shoulder. "Would you stop? He's just a guy."

"A gorgeous talented guy who melts the panties off women everywhere."

I shook my head amused. "You're crazy."

"And you're the luckiest girl I've ever met."

I didn't bother disagreeing with Eliza because she was right. I really was the luckiest girl.

I did, however, block Geoffrey's number. Something I should've done a long time ago.

Kozart

I ended the show with one of our biggest hits, "Archangel." The arena rumbled and the crowd remained on their feet as I made my way offstage, grabbing a water and guzzling it down as I headed backstage.

I stopped short.

Our manager BJ and our publicist Brielle sat on the sofa, their arms crossed and their eyes on mine. BJ was a hefty guy who wore suits with open-collared shirts and no tie. And though some would argue that Brielle had that sexy librarian vibe going with her dark hair pulled back in a tight ponytail and thick-rimmed glasses, I never could get past the stick up her ass.

"What?" I asked, tossing my empty water bottle in a trashcan.

"Have anything you want to tell me?" BJ asked as I grabbed a towel from a nearby stack and wiped my sweaty face.

"Not really," I said, knowing Brielle must've flown in to tell him the news and then speak to me in person rather than continue our conversation via text.

"College girls? Really, Z?" BJ asked holding up an article that read, 'Z's Robbing the Cradle.' "You can have any celebrity you want, but you go after a teenager?"

I leaned my ass against a counter and folded my arms. "My business is my business."

"Not when it affects all of us," Brielle said. "We're a team here, Z. A family. Isn't that what you always tell us?"

I exhaled my exasperation, hating when someone threw my own words back in my face. "She's a senior and twenty-one. And we're just talking," I lied.

"Just talking?" Brielle scoffed. "No girl just wants to *talk* to Z Savage."

"Fuck you, Brielle," I spat as my bandmates filtered into the room.

Their wide eyes told me they'd caught the tail end of what was happening between Brielle, BJ, and me.

"You work for *me*," I spat back at her, not backing down just because we now had an audience. "You don't talk to me like I'm a child."

"Someone needs to give it to you straight," she said.

"What Brielle's trying to say," BJ interrupted, always the diplomat. "Is that you have an image to maintain. No one wants to hear that their favorite rock star is chasing a college girl. Sex, drugs, and rock and roll, man. That's what sells music and merchandise."

My bandmates grabbed some food and drinks and made themselves scarce, knowing when to leave a room to let me handle a situation.

"Your diehard fans wanna hear you're sleeping with some supermodel but keeping it casual," Brielle added. "They don't want their rock star acting like a smitten fool for a college girl."

I clenched my fists, stopping my hands from shaking with fury.

If Brielle wasn't such a hard-working publicist, I would've fired her ass for being so condescending.

"When have you been late to a sound check before today?" she asked. "When have you stayed in another state while your band traveled without you? When have you had a driver take you to a venue and not driven with the band?"

I avoided both of their stares.

"The last few weeks. That's when," she answered for me.

I growled low in my throat, hating that she was right.

"What *you* do affects everyone," Brielle persisted. "And what you did this weekend by flying back to Tennessee was sloppy. Z Savage doesn't do sloppy. Or does he now?"

"Z. The common denominator is this girl," BJ said. "That's all were saying."

"Can you be sure she's not talking to the paparazzi?" Brielle asked.

I glared at her. "She'd never do that."

"How well do you know her?" BJ asked.

I hated that I had to defend my relationship with Aubrey. What we had right now was inexplicable and to hell with whomever wanted me to put it into words. "I'm allowed to have friends outside of the team."

Brielle rolled her eyes. "You've got high-profile companies sponsoring your summer tour. Do you want them pulling out once their rock star's rep is compromised?"

My patience was wearing thin. "That's bullshit and you know it."

She lifted a brow. "Do I?"

Was I really compromising my reputation by dating Aubrey? Did my fans need me single or banging some supermodel? Would my relationship tarnish the reputation I'd worked so hard to create? Or was this just more bullshit Brielle was feeding me to keep me a puppet in my own life? "Do that spinning thing you do," I said to her.

"Oh, I've been working on it," she assured me. "Don't you worry."

"It's about time you earn the money I pay you." I took off for the bus, needing to be away from everyone. I hoped the guys hadn't sought refuge on the bus because I really needed time alone.

Time to think.

Time to calm my fucking nerves.

As soon as I stepped outside the arena, the late September breeze sent a chill over my sweat-covered body. I pushed open the bus door and climbed inside. It was empty.

Thank God.

I stripped down and stepped into the shower. Normally, I reflected on the show. Tonight, I needed to figure out what to do about Brielle and BJ being on my ass about Aubrey. You'd think I'd been caught on video serenading her while holding roses and chocolates.

I'd been seen leaving her place.

Big fucking deal.

This story would disappear like most insignificant news stories did. And then I wouldn't have to listen to them anymore.

CHAPTER NINETEEN

Aubrey

I'd seen the pictures. There was no denying it was Kozart and me. And no one on campus was buying that it wasn't—which made walking across campus a whole new experience.

I grasped the strap on my messenger bag as I headed toward my stuttering class. Heads turned as I passed by. A few people pointed and others whispered.

I kept my eyes down on the walking path and made my way to class. Even as I sat in my back-corner seat, heads turned.

Were the girls wondering how I snagged a rock star? Were they thinking I wasn't good enough or pretty enough for him? And how about the guys? Were they wondering what I'd done—probably in bed—to snag him?

This was why Kozart warned me. He didn't want unnecessary attention on me. But I had a sinking feeling it was too late. Word was out, and people planned to stare.

It could've been worse. They could've been staring because of something I said or did. They were just staring out of curiosity. I got it. I probably would've done the same thing if some girl on campus was dating my favorite country singer. I'd wonder what made her special.

I now understood it wasn't just one thing that made someone special; it was an unspoken attraction. A mutual affection. A common bond. A trust. I wished I could tell everyone that Kozart and I had something you couldn't really explain. Something that had bonded us that first night we shared a bed. Something I didn't even know existed until now.

When class ended, I stuffed my things into my bag, wanting to duck out of class unnoticed.

"Are you really dating Z?" a girl I'd never spoken to before asked.

I opened my mouth to respond, but was cut off by another.

"How do you know him?" the girl who stepped up beside her asked.

"Is he as amazing as he looks?" another asked.

I shrugged. "Don't know him."

"*Right*," they said as I threw my strap across me and stood from my desk.

"Bye," I muttered, unable to get away from them fast enough.

As I crossed campus, I texted Kozart to let him know people were asking questions.

So, you're a celebrity now? He texted back, seemingly unconcerned by the latest turn of events.

Oh, yeah. A total diva.

This will blow over. It'll be fine.

I hoped he was right, because I was the world's worst liar.

CHAPTER TWENTY

Kozart

"What are you doing for your birthday?" Aubrey asked, her voice raspy with sleep since I'd woken her at one in the morning.

"We have a show in Arkansas."

"Yeah, but what will you do to celebrate?"

"Strip club?"

Silence filled the air.

"That was a joke," I explained.

"I knew that," she said, totally not knowing it was a joke.

"Would you care if I went?" I asked, liking the idea of her being upset. Because it meant she wanted me all to herself.

"Why would I care?" she asked, playing stubborn. "Isn't that what rock stars do?"

Stubborn I could take. Assuming I was like everyone else, I couldn't. "I don't like when you say that."

"Say what?"

"That's what rock stars do."

"I'm sorry. I didn't realize—"

"No, it's just, I'd rather you not lump me in with what you hear about other rock stars. I'm hoping you know me better than that now."

She said nothing.

I hoped I hadn't been too abrupt. But just when I thought she was getting to know me better than most, she said something like that which pissed me off. "You there?"

"I'm here," she said. "I'm just...trying to navigate this thing with you. And I'm trying to be...detached, because you're off living your life and I'm living mine. But it's hard."

"I don't want you detached."

"Self-preservation, Kozart. Self-preservation."

Those words haunted me even after we'd hung up. Is that what I'd done to her? Did she feel like she needed to stay on guard at all times so I wouldn't hurt her?

Would I hurt her?

Was I already hurting her?

Aubrey

No longer was I the brunette with the triplets. Now people actually looked past them to see me as I entered a café in the student union. I hated unwarranted attention. And this was times one hundred. Worrying about what people thought of me was the last thing I wanted to be doing. But the looks and whispers were getting to me.

I hadn't mentioned my feelings about it to Kozart because I didn't want him to get angry or to begin worrying about me, but it sucked.

Now I understood, to some extent, what it was like to be him. I mean, obviously his notoriety was through the roof and mine was only campus-wide, but recognition was such a weird thing. I now had to worry about photos being snapped of me and ending up online with a cruel caption. Because fans could be crazy jealous. Especially the ones who believed they had a shot with Kozart.

This made the responsibility of being connected to him even more overwhelming.

I grabbed my lunch and met the girls at a table.

"This is insane," Mandy said.

"What?" Melinda asked.

"Aubrey's celebrity status," Mandy explained, glancing around the room at all the inquisitive eyes.

"I'm not a celebrity," I said, keeping my voice and eyes down.

"You're just sleeping with one," Marla added.

They all giggled and I rolled my eyes.

"When are we actually going to get to meet him?" Melinda asked.

"When the two of you aren't in the middle of a hot make-out session," Mandy added.

Again, they broke into giggles.

If I wasn't so worried about who was eavesdropping or watching us, I probably would've joined in as well. I mean, I was dating a freaking rock star. If I couldn't gossip about it with my girlfriends, what fun was it?

CHAPTER TWENTY-ONE

Aubrey

A few days later, I awoke to a text from Kozart—one he'd written at four in the morning. **What are you doing for the long weekend?**

I wondered if he wasn't able to sleep *or* if he'd never gone to sleep, both notions unsettling me. I texted him back. **Nothing. Where will you be?**

It took a little while, but his text popped up. **Hopefully with you.**

My heart tripped over itself. **What do you have in mind?**

If I send a private jet, will you come to me in New Mexico?

Would I come to him? Did he seriously think I'd say no? **What's in it for me?**

There was no response on his side. No bouncing dots. Nothing.

Did he not realize I was kidding?

Finally, the dots bounced. **Me.**

Butterflies took flight in my belly. That single word was exactly why I'd be on that jet. **Ok.**

Great! I'll send you the details later today.

Ok. Question.

Shoot.

Did you sleep okay last night?

There was no response.

Did he not want to tell me? Was that why he was sending for me? Or did he just really want to see me?

The bouncing dots started up. **I will this weekend.**

My heart clenched. He seriously was going to be the death of me.

The dots began. **Have a great day. I'll talk to you later.**

I responded with a heart and rolled out of bed, ready to start my day while thoughts of our weekend together would undoubtedly fill my mind.

* * *

As promised, a private jet sat by the airport hangar where Kozart instructed me to be for my 7a.m. flight on Saturday morning. A pilot and airport staff greeted me and checked over my license and scanned my bag and backpack before directing me to the set of stairs leading to the jet's open door.

I pulled my small suitcase toward the steps and was met by a young flight attendant.

"Welcome aboard," she said, taking hold of my suitcase. "You ready for your flight to New Mexico?"

I wanted to ask if she knew who I was going to meet. Because if she knew, she wouldn't even have to ask. "Yup."

She led me up the steps and aboard the jet. Once inside, she directed me to a white leather seat with a small table in front of it. "How's this?"

"Great."

She glanced to my suitcase in her hand. "Do you need this or can I stow it for you?"

"No. I've got what I need in my backpack."

She nodded before walking away with it.

As I sat, I surveyed the small aircraft. There were eight white leather seats and two tables. Small oval windows were beside each inside seat.

I looked out my window as I settled in, wondering if anyone else would be joining me. My question was answered when the door closed and the engines whirred to life.

I buckled myself in at the captain's request over the speaker then reached for my earbuds, popping them into my ears to stop the whirring sound from becoming too overpowering. Kozart's voice filled my ears. I dropped my head back against the headrest and closed my eyes, settling in for the two-hour flight. Because of the different time zones, I'd be arriving in New Mexico at 8 a.m., only an hour after I left Tennessee.

Once we took off and reached our cruising altitude, I pulled out my speech disorders book and read the two chapters the professor assigned. I was finding the course so interesting, especially since I knew I'd be needing all the information in the future.

Before long the plane began to descend. An anxious ripple rolled through my stomach. This couldn't be real life. This had to be a dream. Rock stars didn't just date regular girls and send for them whenever they wanted...or did they?

The plane touched down on the runway, bouncing as if it weighed nothing at all. I became even more eager as I watched out the window as the pilot drove us over to another hangar, nowhere near the huge passenger airplanes at the main terminal. When we stopped, I noticed a dark car parked by the hangar and hoped Kozart was inside.

The door to the jet slowly opened. Out the window, I watched the flight attendant carry my bag down the steps and roll it over to the car. Arthur stood by the trunk, awaiting my luggage. Sadness swept over me. That wasn't the familiar face I hoped to be seeing.

I unbuckled myself and stood from my seat, brushing any wrinkles out of my sleeveless pink blouse and jeans before grabbing my backpack. I made my way to the open door and waved to Arthur as I stepped out onto the top step. The New Mexico heat engulfed me, stealing away my breath, as Arthur waved back.

"Don't I get a hello?"

My eyes shot to the bottom of the steps. Kozart stood there in khaki cargo shorts, a white T-shirt, a backward ball cap, and a cocky grin.

I rushed down the steps, throwing myself into his arms. He lifted me right off my feet, his big arms wrapping tightly around me as he buried his nose into my hair. I couldn't tell whose heart beat faster since they both pounded like jackhammers.

"I've missed your smell," he said.

I pulled back with pinched brows. *"That's* what you missed?"

He chuckled. "And your face."

"Keep going," I smirked.

"And you in my T-shirt."

"How about my glowing personality?" I sassed.

"And that."

"How about—"

His lips sealed over mine, cutting off my words. I didn't care that anyone else was around. I fell into the kiss, breathing him in and wanting to be as close to him as possible as our tongues did a frantic dance on the tarmac.

"Ahem," Arthur said, clearing his throat.

Our kiss turned into the two of us smiling before finally pulling apart.

"We can continue that in the car," Kozart said, placing me on my feet and linking his fingers with mine. "I'm happy you're here," he said as we walked to the car.

I squeezed his hand. "Me too."

"Hello," Arthur greeted me as we stepped up to the open back door.

"Hi, Arthur. It's nice to see you again," I said before sliding inside the backseat first.

Arthur grinned. "Same."

"I love him," I said once the door closed and Kozart sat beside me.

"He's a good man," Kozart agreed as he slipped his arm across the back of my shoulders then pulled me into his side. "I've missed touching you."

"Oh, here we go," I teased.

He leaned over and gently coaxed my lips apart with his tongue. I let him kiss me slow and gentle. Our first kiss on the tarmac was rushed and desperate. This one was him realizing I wasn't going anywhere. Before I knew it, he'd pulled me into his lap so I straddled him. Our kiss became more intense as his tongue dove deeper, moving with purpose as his hands grabbed my ass.

I finally pulled back, breathless and beyond turned on. Based on the bulge in his cargo shorts, he was just as turned on as I was. "What are we doing today?"

A slow smile tugged up one corner of his mouth. "Funny you should ask. We're headed there right now."

My brows shot up. "Oh yeah?"

He nodded.

"Do you have a show tonight?"

He shook his head. "I'm all yours."

Was that truly the case?

He eventually shifted me off his lap. I slid into the spot beside him as we drove the remainder of the way to our destination, his arm around me and my body tucked into his side. I'd missed his just-showered scent and the safety his arms provided. Talking on the phone and texting worked, but there was nothing like breathing the same air as Kozart.

Arthur turned off the main road and onto a dirt road. The uneven terrain bounced us all over the back seat. When the car finally pulled to a stop, I glanced out my window. We were the only car in a dirt parking lot. Confused, I looked out Kozart's window. That's when I saw it. A giant Ferris wheel, aglow with flashing lights as it spun around. And even though it was broad daylight, the big colorful bulbs still would've given even the most serious adult a case of nostalgia.

I looked to Kozart.

He was grinning. "They opened just for us."

My mouth formed an O. "Just for us?"

He nodded as he pushed open his door. He stepped out and extended his hand back in for me. "Come on."

I took his hand and slid out of the car. He led me through the entranceway. As we made our way down the gangway, workers stood at the numerous food stands. The smells of popcorn, cotton candy, and fried dough floated through the air.

We continued on, moving by the game booths. Unlike a carnival that was opened to the public, the workers didn't shout to us, trying to lure us to their games. They let us pass, knowing we had our pick of activities.

Kozart didn't make eye contact with any of them, but I couldn't help but smile and nod to them to acknowledge we appreciated them being there for us.

Kozart led me to the rides. All of them moved, their lights flashing and whimsical organ music accompanying them. He stopped at the Ferris wheel. "Do you mind heights?"

I shook my head. "Love them."

The worker pulled his lever and we waited as the ride slowly came to a stop. Once a car sat at the bottom, he pulled open the front bar and let us slide in before securing the bar across our laps. "Just let me know when you've had enough," the worker said.

Kozart nodded as he grabbed my hand and off we went, slowly moving upward. As we reached the top, we had a full view of the carnival spread out over the middle of nowhere.

"This is very cool," I said.

"The Ferris wheel?"

"Having the whole place to ourselves. Is it easier for you if no one else is here?"

"Yeah, and I kinda just wanted you to myself doing something fun."

The Ferris wheel made a full rotation, and then we were being lifted back up and over the top again. "Did you get to go to carnivals as a kid?"

He shook his head. "I always wondered what it'd be like, you know, when I saw them in movies or TV."

"When did you go to your first one?"

He chuckled.

I bumped him with my shoulder. "What?"

"This is my first one."

"Liar."

"No, I'm serious." And he was. I could see it in the serious creases around his eyes.

"Oh my God. Then we've got to do everything. Eat lots of cotton candy and candy apples and ride every ride like fifty times."

He leaned over and kissed me hard.

"What was that for?" I asked.

"For being you. I always know what I'm getting and I can't seem to get enough."

I basked in the feel of his words, trying to stifle the giant grin that tugged away at my lips. "I love that you took me here. And I love that I'm with you for one of your firsts."

He smiled and I knew he loved that he could give me this, too. He'd done a lot with other girls, but he'd never done *this* with any of them. *This* was all mine.

We spent the afternoon riding every ride at the carnival and eating sugary junk food. Knowing the carnival would be opening in the evening for the public, Kozart began to get fidgety.

"Do we need to get going?" I asked, as we walked around sharing the pink cotton candy I held.

"Not yet," he said, grabbing a fluffy wad and popping it into his mouth.

"I like that I get to see this side of you."

He gave me a sidelong glance. "You know what *I* like?"

"What?"

"I used to hate all my memories."

My face scrunched, confused by his words.

"But I'm starting to have more good memories than bad ones," he explained.

"That's good."

"That's damn good," he assured me.

"Any bridesmaids in those memories?"

He chuckled. "Just one."

My brows shot up. "Memory?"

"Bridesmaid."

I smiled, before my eyes snagged on something. "The balloon game," I said, moving us toward the game with the wall of colorful balloons.

"What do you need to do?" Kozart asked me.

My brows shot up. "You really don't know?"

"I assume you need to pop them."

"With a dart," I said, hating his parents for choosing drugs and a life of crime over him. Did they know how amazing he turned out? Did they know he'd made it without them?

We stepped up to the counter and the worker placed three darts down in front of Kozart.

He grabbed the darts and threw the first one, popping a red balloon. He threw the second one, popping a green balloon.

"You're good at this," I said.

He looked to me. "I'm good at everything."

I rolled my eyes.

"No, seriously. It's what happens when you spend too much time in bars playing pool and darts."

"So, you're a ringer?"

He laughed. "Something like that." He threw his final dart and popped a yellow balloon.

The worker motioned toward the row of small stuffed animals at the bottom of the wall. "You've got your pick of these."

Kozart's eyes shot up to the big stuffed animals hanging from the ceiling. "What do I need to do to win one of those?"

"Pop ten balloons," the man said.

"Which one do you want?" Kozart asked me.

"I don't need a giant gorilla. I'm fine with one of the small ones."

He cocked his head. "Yeah?"

"I'm easy to please."

His brows bounced. "I know."

I shoved his shoulder and he laughed as he pointed to a small stuffed animal. "I'll take that one."

"The frog?" I asked as he turned and handed it to me. "Why not the rabbit?"

"Well...you were kissing a frog before you met me. And I want you to remember, not all frogs are bad."

I smiled as I hugged it to me. "I love my frog."

He swallowed down hard.

Oh, shit. Had I just told him I loved him?

Shit. Shit. Shit

"I just meant...I didn't mean I...thank you. For winning it for me. And for taking me here," I said, hoping I hadn't scared him off.

"I know what you meant," he said, wrapping his arm around me and walking us toward the exit.

But did he know? Because I sure didn't.

* * *

Kozart and I lay tangled in the hotel sheets. My head lay on his bare chest as he held my open textbook. "Spasmodic Dysphonia?"

I knew that one. "Spasming of the vocal chords when someone speaks. Their voice could be described as shaky or hoarse."

"You got it," he said. "How about Dysarthria?"

I thought for a minute. "That's caused by muscle damage to the diaphragm, lips, tongue, and vocal chords. It results in slurred or slowed speech. Also, changes in voice quality."

"Yup. You got it." He closed the book and tossed it down. "You're really smart, you know that?"

"Why do I get the feeling you're going to somehow bring this back to me choosing to date you?"

He laughed. "No, it's refreshing, that's all."

"What?"

"Being around someone who knows so much. Everyone I'm around just wants to talk music. Me and you. Our conversations are so much more interesting."

"Until you put out your next album and I give you my honest opinion."

He grinned as he twisted me onto my back and lay on top of me. "I value your opinion."

"We'll see."

"What do you think about me coming to your graduation?"

My eyes widened, unprepared for the subject change. "Do you want to come to my graduation?"

"Of course. You've seen me on stage. I want to be there to see you on stage."

"It's in May."

"What are you saying? You plan to get rid of me before May?" he asked with a grin.

"No, I just meant isn't that when your summer tour begins?"

He shook his head. "It starts in June. I'll be at your graduation. Clapping the loudest."

CHAPTER TWENTY-TWO
Kozart

Cell phone lights lit up the dark arena like stars in the night sky as I sang my final song. Moments like these made me want to pinch myself. Was this really my life? Were these people really all here to see me? Like I'd told Aubrey, the crowd singing my songs never got old.

The band continued to play even after I sang the final verse—my cue to end the show.

"Thanks for coming out to see us, Dallas! We hope to see you again real soon!" I raised a fist in the air and walked offstage, grabbing a water from the speaker and chugging it.

"Have fun at your carnival?" Brielle asked as soon as I stepped backstage.

My eyes narrowed on her standing there with her arms crossed and BJ beside her. "What?"

"Don't play coy, Z. It doesn't suit you," she said, holding up her phone.

I inched closer so I could see her screen. A photo of Aubrey and me eating cotton candy as we strolled through the carnival this past weekend was clear as day. *Fuck.* "Where'd you get that?"

"The question is, where can't I get it? It's everywhere," she said. "What the hell were you thinking?"

"It was only opened for us. No one else was there."

She scoffed. "Did the staff sign NDAs?"

"What?"

"Did they agree not to talk or take pictures?" she asked, the condescension dripping from every word.

"No, I—"

"You didn't know because it's not your job to arrange things like this," she said. "That's what your team is here for. We make sure photos like these never see the light of day."

My eyes cast down as I tried reigning in my anger. I was a grown man. I didn't need to be reprimanded. But, as much as it pained me to admit it, Brielle was right. I didn't think to have the workers sign anything. I just knew no one else would be there and that was enough for me.

"Z, you've been going rogue lately," BJ chimed in. "What's it gonna take for you to understand?"

"Understand what?"

"The endorsements? The merchandise? The brand?" he said. "You mess it up, you mess it up for *all* of us."

"I'm allowed to spend time with girls."

Brielle shook her head, exasperation written all over her face.

"Z?"

My head shot behind me. My band had joined us in the room.

"Dude, we're all for you getting laid," Treyton said. "But you gotta know by now that seventy-five percent of our revenue comes from females. And I'd like to say they're here to see me. But we all know why they're really here."

Heat crept up my neck and my fist clenched around my water bottle. Were my bandmates really siding with them?

"It's not like this relationship's serious or anything," Camden added. "Everyone knows you're not a one-woman kind of guy."

Was that what they thought of me? Did they really think I was incapable of falling for someone?

"Yeah, dude," Treyton added. "Why let this temporary thing ruin what we've built?"

"You really think me having someone in my life is temporary?" I asked, stunned he'd support this craziness.

He cocked his head, amused. "Dude."

I leveled him with my eyes. Out of everyone, we'd been through the most together. He'd give it to me straight. "You seriously think this could ruin us?"

"Let's just keep riding this high out," he said. "Why mess with it now? We've made it to the mother fucking top with a single lead singer."

"One who can play into these women's fantasies," Brielle added. "Don't you get it, Z? These women actually think they have a shot with you. If they see you as taken, they'll lose interest and find some other band."

My head began to spin. My pulse rattled like a pinball in my temples. What the fuck was going on? Was this an intervention? Did they really want me to stop seeing Aubrey? My eyes flicked to each of the traitors. "So, that's how you all feel?"

Knowing I was pissed, my bandmates avoided my eyes while Brielle and BJ nodded vehemently.

Without a word, I turned and took off for the exit. I needed to get the hell away from them. All of them.

Reggie saw me coming and held open the door.

Arthur was seated behind the steering wheel of the car and tried to jump out once he saw me, but I gave him no time, throwing open the back door and climbing inside. I slouched in my seat, pissed, hurt, and hating everyone in that room.

"Where to?" Arthur asked through the rearview mirror.

"Anywhere but here."

He nodded.

My phone rang on the seat beside me. I ignored it. I couldn't believe Treyton didn't have my back. *None* of them did. My phone continued ringing. Knowing I couldn't talk to any of them feeling the way I did, I grabbed it to silence it. But it wasn't them. It was Aubrey.

I closed my eyes, not wanting to answer, but not wanting to ignore her either. I released a long breath and answered it. "Hey."

"Happy Birthday!!!!"

The sound of Aubrey's excited voice momentarily made me forget how pissed off I was—and that it was midnight which meant it was technically my birthday.

"Tell me I'm the first one to wish you a happy birthday," she said.

"You're definitely the first," I assured her, trying to sound upbeat while I really wanted to jump out of my own skin.

"I like being your first—and yes, I'm counting every ride at the carnival individually."

Fuck me. She *was* my first everything these days.

I wished my band could see how amazing she was and how damn happy she made me, even when I was at my lowest.

"How was your show?" she asked.

"Better if you were there."

"Oh, you're good," she said, always assuming I was giving her a line.

"Where's my frog?" I asked.

"*My* frog. And he's right next to me," she said.

"I kinda like that."

"Me, too."

"I wish it were me."

"Me, too."

The more I spoke to her, the angrier I became—the complete opposite of how I should've been feeling hearing her voice. She didn't deserve my anger. She didn't deserve my team's animosity toward everything she represented. "Thanks for being the first to call. But I know you have that stuttering test tomorrow, so I'll let you get some sleep," I said, trying to end the call before I said something I shouldn't.

She gasped. "Are you trying to get rid of me so you can go to a strip club?"

"What? No. The strip club's tomorrow night on my actual birthday."

She laughed, and I loved how easily I could amuse her. Up until tonight, everything had been so easy between us, except of course the distance. That would never get easy. But I'd been trying, and she'd been receptive, jumping on a plane at short notice to come to me. I loved that about her.

"Well, have a great day tomorrow," she said. "Maybe you can call me before you head out to see the strippers."

"They prefer exotic dancers."

She laughed, and everything about the sweet sound made me hate my team for wanting to take away the one thing that made me happy.

"Good night, country girl."

"Night, rock god," she said before disconnecting the call.

I sat there, staring at my phone's blank screen, contemplating what I needed to do. Could I really get through the day without talking to her or texting her? Could I let her go because I was being persuaded to do so…by everyone? Could I ever feel this way about another woman?

Fuck this.

"Take me to a bar," I called to Arthur.

His disappointed eyes met mine in the rearview mirror.

I didn't pay him to be disappointed. I fucking paid him to get me from place to place without any questions.

Two hours later I sat alone in the corner of a deserted dive bar. The bartender, sick of serving me whiskey shots every two minutes, handed me the bottle. I tossed a hundred-dollar bill on the bar and drank right from the bottle.

Before long, the room began to spin and the music drifting from the old jukebox on the wall became muffled. I was shit-faced and free. Free from Brielle. Free from BJ. And free from my traitor bandmates.

CHAPTER TWENTY-THREE

Kozart

I stepped out of the shower backstage after our show in Arkansas. I pulled on jeans, a T-shirt, and my hat. I stepped outside to Arthur, standing by the open back door of the car.

"Z?"

My eyes cut to the tour bus parked nearby.

Treyton jogged toward me. "Dude. What are we doing to celebrate your birthday?"

My eyes narrowed on his. "I wanna be alone."

He tilted his head as Arthur walked away, leaving us to it. "Come on. Don't you think you've given us all enough silent treatment today?"

"I'll say when it's been enough."

"That's fucked up," he said.

"You know what's fucked up? You not having my back with BJ and Brielle. You knowing I had a shitty life—just like you—and not being happy when I was finally happy. You knowing it's a rare fucking thing for me to wanna invest time in someone and you telling me to cut her loose. You seeing dollar signs over my mother-fucking happiness." I shook my head in disgust, knowing when I needed to be away from a situation. I slipped in the car and slammed the door, never so happy to be away from my oldest friend.

* * *

"Happy fucking birthday to me," I said before tossing back another shot. Tonight's bar was a little more crowded, but I'd been seated in my own booth in the corner of the room, away from prying eyes. The problem with that was I was drunk as a skunk and attracting attention with my big mouth.

My phone vibrated on the table. Aubrey's name lit up my screen. I wondered if she was checking if I'd gone to sleep after my show or if I'd actually gone to a strip club. It didn't matter. I sent the call to voicemail. Nothing good could come from speaking to her in my condition.

Arthur stepped into the bar a little while later. "You ready?" he asked, more of a suggestion than a question.

"Do you think I need to be single?" I asked him, slurring like the pissed off drunk I was.

"I'm not sure I know what you mean."

I rolled out of the booth, not even close to smoothly, and staggered toward the exit with Arthur behind me. I pushed open the door and tripped over the step leading outside. Had Arthur's hand not shot out and caught me, I would've face-planted on the concrete sidewalk. Once I stood upright, I looked him in the eyes. "You think I should cut Aubrey loose, too?"

His eyes narrowed as he pulled open the car door for me. "Why would you do that?"

"Because I'm supposed to be single."

"Says who?"

I slid inside the backseat. "Every-fucking-one."

Arthur stood on the sidewalk looking in at me. "What do *you* want?"

I shrugged. "I just wanna be happy."

He nodded sadly. "Then I guess you need to do what makes you happy."

"It's never that easy." My phone vibrated and I tipped the screen to see it. Aubrey again.

"She makes it easy," Arthur said, nodding toward Aubrey's name on my screen.

I sent the call to voicemail then my eyes shot to his. "Huh?"

"I've never seen you as happy as you are when you're around her."

Before I could respond, he slammed the door.

I assumed he wanted his words to permeate. He wanted me to realize he was right. He wanted me to stop being such an asshole.

Aubrey

An icy chill rushed through me as soon as Kozart sent my phone call to voicemail. I lay on my bed in complete darkness wearing his T-shirt, wanting to feel close to him on his birthday—even though I hadn't spoken to him since midnight. And now he was blowing off my calls.

Too many bad images flashed through my mind. Kozart at strip clubs. Kozart with groupies. I had no idea how he'd even spent his birthday. And when we *had* spoken at midnight, he seemed off. I didn't want to press him, so I just acted like everything was fine. But I could tell something was on his mind.

Maybe the distance was getting to him. Or maybe he'd seen the pictures of us from the carnival and it pissed him off. Maybe this just wasn't working for him anymore. I'd be lying if I said the thoughts didn't twist a knot in my stomach.

God. Was I being needy? Couldn't he just hang with his friends and not have to call me every night? Couldn't that just be okay and not a situation that had me questioning him? Questioning us?

I grabbed my pillow and pressed it over my face, needing to get a grip. If I was going to be in this relationship, I needed to trust him. I needed to believe what we had was real. I needed to trust that he wouldn't be out doing unthinkable things. Things that would break my heart.

The muffled sound of my phone pinging pricked my ears a little while later.

I tossed aside the pillow and grabbed it.

Kozart texted. **Do you trust me?**

My nose wrinkled. Was he really a mind reader? Had he heard my internal ramblings again? **Of course.**

I'm gonna need you to prove it.

What? **Are you drunk? You're not making any sense.**

A long time passed before his response appeared. **Promise me.**

Promise him? Something was definitely wrong with him. I should have asked him about it last night. I responded the only way I could. **Promise.**

Good night, country girl.

My thumbs sent off a reply. **Happy Birthday, Kozart. Sleep well.**

He didn't return my text. Deep down I knew he wouldn't.

His cryptic question would undoubtedly keep me up all night. What did he plan to do that warranted my trust? Why hadn't he called me? Was he in a noisy place? Was he partying? Was he too drunk?

Ughhhhh.

I wished I'd heard his voice. I would've been able to read him. I'd know things were okay.

Maybe I was just being irrational and untrusting. The exact opposite of what I'd just promised him.

I lay in bed wishing two things. One, that I didn't have such a big surprise for him that I was now second-guessing. And two, that his text didn't feel like him telling me something I didn't want to hear.

CHAPTER TWENTY-FOUR

Aubrey

"Do you think he'll let us backstage?" Melinda asked from the driver's seat as we crossed state lines into Mississippi.

"Will he introduce us to the rest of the band?" Eliza asked from the back seat squished between Mandy and Marla.

"The point of it being a surprise is not telling him we're coming," I said, staring out my passenger seat window and hoping this was a good surprise. His last text had left me feeling uneasy and I hadn't spoken to him today. But the girls and I planned this a while ago. And I couldn't back out now. I'd initially tried to get tickets to his actual birthday show in Arkansas, but it was sold out. So, the following night in Mississippi was the next best thing.

"This is gonna be so amazing," Marla said, passing us red licorice from the backseat.

I grabbed one, excited yet nervous to be surprising Kozart. I couldn't wait to see his face, especially when I gave him his birthday gift.

"You know, if this wasn't a surprise we could've had front row seats," Mandy said.

The whole car groaned, knowing we definitely could have.

"Next time," I assured them.

An hour later, we pulled into the crowded parking lot. The sun had set and groups of people walked in droves toward the arena. Kozart's face was plastered on the fronts of many T-shirts. Women had taken liberties and torn their shirts in provocative places.

Melinda found a spot and we parked. My excitement began to set in. I knew he liked to change things up, so I wondered what he had planned for his Mississippi fans.

We stepped out of the car, stretching our legs for the first time in hours. Kozart's voice blared from several cars. Some blasted his louder songs while some preferred his ballads. We followed the sea of bodies moving to the arena with our tickets in hand.

Once inside the building, my eyes were drawn to the merchandise tables. Shirts, hats, and even pajamas were displayed on the faux wall. Tons of people waited in lines to make their purchases. I was seeing it from a different perspective this time. No longer did I sit in the front row and get escorted to the back. Now I was in the midst of his fans. Many were already wasted, some carrying their overpriced cups of beer happily, while some who'd partied pre-concert spilled their drinks as they moved through the packed crowd.

"I'm getting a shirt," Eliza announced as she pushed her way through groups of people to get to one of the merchandise stands.

Mandy followed her. "Me, too."

"You want a drink?" Melinda asked me. "You look like you could use one."

"I'm just excited. That's all." And I was. But I wasn't going to lie and say I wasn't a little nervous to see his reaction.

We all met back up at our seats in the upper level of the arena. We had a view of the entire place: the stage, the quickly filling seats, and all the screens that would bring Kozart up close and personal with every fan in the room.

The lights flickered on and off and the crowd cheered.

An announcer's voice echoed through the room pointing out the exits in the building.

The shadows of Kozart's bandmates walked across the stage.

A roar ran through the crowd.

My friends all looked excitedly to me.

The drums began and then the guitars.

The noise from the crowd grew louder.

The lights on stage flashed on and Kozart stood behind the mic at center stage.

Earth-shaking screams spread through the arena. My friends' screams were lost in the mix and I could only stand there and watch the craziness. Being so far away from the stage, I couldn't see Kozart's face. I could only watch it on screen. His knowing smirk slipped into place as he allowed the screaming to go on for a little bit before gripping the mic and belting out the lyrics to his first number one hit.

My body buzzed at the sight of him. My fingers itched to touch him. I was pretty certain every woman in that arena felt the same way. The difference was I'd actually touched him and planned to again tonight.

By the second song, the noise in the arena had died down slightly. And by the third, he started into my favorite song. The screen on stage scanned the audience as he sang, focusing on groups of girls singing the words at the top of their lungs. It moved to what seemed to be the front row. Phoebe Larsen, an A list actress, sat there. Her face on the screen sent up a muffled roar in the crowd. She smiled coyly, probably hating the fact that she'd been outed at the concert. Her image was replaced by Kozart's as he finished the song.

Multiple songs ensued, and the crowd seemed to be loving every one of them—and every minute of the two-hour show.

"Midnight," his biggest hit was the song that always closed the show. So, the moment I heard the music begin, I texted him. **I have a surprise for you.**

I motioned for my friends to follow me so we could make our way to the lower level and backstage. When Kozart sang his final note, we were out in the concourse, but we stepped down to the lower level just as he exited the stage. His band continued playing for another minute, then they slapped the hands of fans in the front row.

Finally, the house lights switched on and everyone filed out of their seats. We walked against the tide of bodies going in the opposite direction of us. We eventually reached the front row.

Kozart's bodyguard stood in front of the entryway to backstage. Since a barrier prohibited anyone from getting too close to the entry, I waved over to him, trying to get his attention. His eyes shot away from mine, but I could've sworn he saw me.

"Reggie!" I called.

His eyes continued to avert mine, though there was no way he couldn't hear me.

"Hey, Buddy!" Mandy yelled.

That got his attention. He begrudgingly walked over, but didn't say a word.

As the crowd around me dispersed, the gift dropped from my hand and my shaking legs threatened to give out. Arms from all directions cocooned me.

"He's not worth it," Mandy said as she squeezed me tightly.

"You can do so much better," Marla assured me.

"I'm never listening to his music again," Eliza promised.

"Come on," Mandy said, turning me away from the hotel, the crowd, and the memory of what once was.

"Melinda's in the car ready to get us the hell away from this place," Marla said.

As if in the midst of a nightmare, I said nothing as we returned to the car. I slipped into the backseat, letting Mandy have the front. We were supposed to stay over, getting a room at the same hotel as Kozart, but they knew better than to make me go in there.

My head whirled as we drove through the night. I actually pinched myself to check if I was asleep. I wasn't.

I always knew this thing between Kozart and me was on borrowed time. I always knew he'd be tempted by other women, including celebrities. I just didn't know I'd have a front row seat to it. I didn't think he'd be so careless with my feelings.

"Did he call?" Eliza whispered.

I shrugged, my head against the cool window.

"Want me to check?" she offered.

I shook my head, now realizing why his bodyguard wouldn't let me backstage. He had another girl there. Someone famous. Someone more fitting for him.

190 | J . N a t h a n

By the time we arrived home, a little after four in the morning, I climbed out of the backseat with Eliza. "So much for a girls' trip," I said, meaning it as an apology for making them drive all that way to Mississippi just to turn around and drive back a couple hours later.

"Don't you dare do that," Mandy warned. "He did this. Not you."

I nodded, wishing that could somehow mend my broken heart. "Thanks for going with me," I said, before turning and walking to the door.

Eliza let us in, probably realizing my shaking hands wouldn't be able to get the key in the lock.

Once inside, I said good night to Eliza and climbed into my bed fully clothed. It was only then I finally allowed the tears to fall.

I *knew* better.

I knew better than to think a rock star would change for me. I knew he couldn't be trusted. He's the one who told me so in the beginning, confirming it even still last night. I just didn't want to hear him.

That was on me.

CHAPTER TWENTY-FIVE

Kozart

After showing Phoebe to her room in the penthouse, I dropped down onto the sofa and buried my face in my hands. *What the hell was I doing?*

I'd walked Phoebe to the elevator after we'd had a couple drinks in the bar. I made sure the paparazzi got their pictures, throwing my arm around her for good measure as we entered the elevator together. I definitely checked my phone too many times to be considered polite during drinks, but Phoebe didn't seem to mind.

I just wished I knew what Aubrey's message meant about a surprise for me. She never followed it up with another text.

I needed to text her. I needed to let her know what was happening. I promised to be honest with her if this thing had run its course. But all of this with Phoebe just happened so fast.

A knock on the penthouse door pulled my attention to it. In no mood for visitors, I tried to ignore it. But when the knocking persisted, I jumped to my feet and trudged to it, checking the peephole to see who I needed to ream out.

Reggie stood outside. He knew better than to bother me. I yanked open the door.

He extended a tall gift bag to me. "This had your name on it."

I took the bag from him, surprised by the unexpected weight of it. "Where'd it come from?"

"It was outside the hotel."

I checked the tag and my stomach churned, my head spinning like an out-of-control carnival ride. This wasn't happening. This wasn't fucking happening. "Was she...?"

He nodded. "But she's gone now."

"What do you mean she's gone?"

He cocked his head. He'd seen me with Phoebe backstage. He'd escorted us upstairs. He thought I was a dick. And Aubrey must think the same now, too.

"Fuuuuuck," I growled.

He pulled the door closed, leaving me to deal with the consequences of my actions.

I walked to the sofa on unsteady legs, dropping down once again. Why the hell hadn't she told me she was coming? Why surprise me?

Surprise?

Fuck.

She did try to tell me.

I glanced to the gift bag. What had she done?

I dug my hands inside the bag, pushing aside the tissue paper. "*Fuuuuuuck!*" I roared as my hands flew out of the bag, as if the gift would detonate if I touched it.

"Z?" Phoebe asked, stepping out of her room in tiny black lingerie. "You okay?"

I didn't even fucking care that this hot actress stood before me partially naked. All I could see was what was in the bag. "Yeah. I just need to be alone for a bit."

She nodded and turned back into the room, her ass hanging out of her thong as she did.

The sight of the gift twisted a knot in my gut. Who was I kidding? It tore my heart right out of my chest leaving a gaping hole.

But I was a big boy. I'd made my bed. Now I needed to sleep in it.

I dug both hands back into the bag and pulled out the gift.

A skateboard.

A *fucking* skateboard.

My head dropped back into the sofa cushions as I held the skateboard in my lap. If I could've made myself disappear into the cushions, I would've.

Aubrey knew me.

She fucking *knew* me. And what did I do? I let everyone else get into my head.

I'd been pulled in two different directions. The way I felt for Aubrey and my loyalty to the people who helped me get to where I was.

I needed to be loyal to both, but I couldn't.

I just fucking couldn't.

There was no way I could call Aubrey now. There was no way I could make any of this right. She'd left the gift, which meant she already knew. She already made up her mind about me. About us.

Dammit.

Though I hadn't planned on Aubrey being here for Phoebe and my coming out party, I'd asked her to trust me. And she hadn't.

I think down deep I always knew she couldn't completely trust me. Not wholeheartedly anyway. At the first sign of me straying, she was gone. Gone without hearing me out. Gone without giving me the benefit of the doubt. Gone without even saying goodbye.

I guess it told me where I really stood with Aubrey.

I shouldn't have been surprised by her not trusting me.

I shouldn't have been surprised that she gave up on me.

It was the story of my life.

CHAPTER TWENTY-SIX

Aubrey

Concealed by night, I jogged across campus. I jogged like it was something I enjoyed. Something that rejuvenated me. But I *hated* jogging. I hadn't done it since rehabbing my knee from my gymnastics' injury freshmen year in high school, but I just couldn't take being in my room any longer. The silence suffocated me, and I needed to breathe. I needed to be alone without Eliza peeking in on me every half an hour. I needed to clear my head. I needed to just be.

Sweat dripped down the sides of my face. My ponytail bounced as my steps mirrored the rap music drifting through my wireless earbuds. I listened to nothing that could cue up Kozart's music, or worse, country music—for fear of hearing *my* song.

God. How could I have been so wrong about him? How could I have gotten played for a fool for a second time?

I was smarter than that.

Better than that.

But it hurt. It hurt so damn badly.

And how could he not have the decency to call me? Was me seeing him with her enough of an explanation in his mind? Had they been together this whole time, and I was just too stupid to see it? Was that why he warned me? Asked if I trusted him? Was it reverse psychology, and he was really telling me not to trust him?

I tried to stay off the internet. I really did. But my friends kept begging me not to go online and that only intensified my curiosity. They had been right to warn me. I couldn't escape the story of the rock star and Hollywood's sweetheart. A story didn't get juicier than that. And, of course, there were pictures. A boatload of pictures of him looking at her like he couldn't live without her. I'd been on the receiving end of that look for what I now realized was only the blink of an eye. Even the way he touched her in the pictures was the same way he'd touched me. I hadn't been special.

Had he told her he needed *her* to sleep too?

The thought pressed me to run harder, pushing myself to my limits until I couldn't do it anymore. I stopped somewhere in the middle of campus, bending at the knees and grasping my thighs, gasping for much needed air.

How was I going to hold my head up high on campus?

How was I not going to let this bring me down?

How was I ever going to get over Kozart Savage?

My phone pinged in my armband. I slipped it out, hating myself for hoping it was him. Hoping he'd explain himself. Hoping there was a good reason behind it all.

Where are you? Eliza texted.

I exhaled my disappointment and texted her back. **Be home soon.** I tucked my phone back into my armband and took off for home before she sent out a search party.

CHAPTER TWENTY-SEVEN

Kozart

The spotlight blinded me as I sang acoustically alone on stage. My sleepless nights were catching up with me. Every word I sang made me vulnerable. Any slip-up would be noticeable to the crowd. But they cheered me on, singing along to the cover I'd chosen for tonight.

I knew they were there to hear *our* music, but there was something about singing a popular song everyone knew. Those types of unexpected live moments always brought the house down.

When my final words echoed through the arena, the crowd—the ones who weren't already standing—jumped to their feet.

The spotlight switched off and I sat in complete darkness as twenty-thousand fans let me know how awesome I was. Too bad *I* knew the truth. Knew how difficult it was to look in the mirror every day. Knew how difficult it was to have other people depend on me for their livelihoods.

"Thank you! Good night, Chicago!" I called to the crowd, before walking offstage. I'd been ending the show differently each night, which pissed the hell out of my audio-visual guys and the crew, but this was my show. I was gonna do it how I saw fit.

I stepped backstage to an empty room, reveling in the silence for just a minute. Soon, the room would be filled with my band, big wigs from management, and some mega-fans who won a personalized meet-and-greet with me and the guys.

Suddenly, my throat constricted and I couldn't breathe.

I twisted around, searching for a place to disappear. Tell me I wasn't having a fucking panic attack. I spotted a door in the corner of the room and headed toward it.

"Z," BJ called.

Fuck.

I inhaled a deep breath and released it keeping the panic attack in check. I swung back around, trying to refrain from looking like I'd just been on the verge of losing it.

"I wanted you to see who was at the show tonight," he said as he walked toward me with a bunch of guys in suits. "You remember Joe, Mark, and Steve."

I nodded, having no clue who they were. "Yeah, of course, good seeing you."

"Awesome show, Z," one of them said. "Looking forward to sponsoring the tour this summer."

I smiled. Sponsors. Got it. "It's gonna be amazing."

One of them held out a gift bag with their liquor company's logo on it. "This is for you."

Thoughts of another gift bag flashed before my eyes and a cold chill ran up my spine.

"Just a little something to get you started," he said.

I took the bag from him. It was heavy and I knew what was inside. "Thank you." My eyes flashed around the suddenly crowded room. "Listen, I've gotta get a shower before this place fills up any more. It was great to see you, and I'm looking forward to seeing you guys overseas this summer."

They said their goodbyes, and I turned away, hurrying for the door now more eager than ever to get away.

"Z," Brielle called.

I continued walking, pretending not to hear her.

"Z! Your fans are waiting to meet you," she persisted.

Fuck.

I stopped, knowing I had obligations, especially to the fans who supported me and gave me my life.

But I just needed a minute.

One fucking minute.

I closed my eyes, doing what I always did. Pleased everyone else.

I turned around and forced a smile. A group of about ten girls stood with Brielle across the room, beaming like they'd just won the lottery. I'd like to say the looks never got old, but they did. Probably because I knew I wasn't the guy they thought I was. I wasn't the guy *I* thought I was.

I pulled the bottle of whiskey out of the gift bag and unscrewed it, tipping it back and taking a nice long swig. Something needed to get me through this night.

Brielle stared me down, giving me 'Don't fuck this up' eyes.

I downed another swig before walking over to the eager fans. "Hey, ladies. What'd you think of the show?"

They all gushed over how amazing it was.

I lifted a brow at Brielle. See? I was a true performer.

CHAPTER TWENTY-EIGHT

Aubrey

I grasped my messenger bag strap as I entered class, as if it could somehow protect me from the prying eyes. It couldn't. The quiet chatter in the classroom turned to silence as soon as I stepped inside. They'd all been talking about me. I understood. Kozart's face had been strewn all over the internet with a famous actress.

I caught the eyes of the three girls who'd cornered me about Kozart when the first photo of us went viral. I assumed they'd give me the pity frown I'd been getting from everyone else, but their lips curved up. And they whispered to one another.

Were they really happy about my misfortune?

Did they really not care how embarrassed I must've felt?

Because, I wouldn't wish the type of despair I was feeling on my worst enemy.

* * *

The sound of banging on the front door after eleven sent Eliza running into my room.

"Grab your mace!" she said.

"Murderers don't knock," I assured her as I tossed my book on my bed and stepped into the hallway.

We moved to our front door.

"Who is it?" Eliza asked through the door.

"Us," the triplets replied.

I rolled my eyes at the over-reactor beside me and pulled open the door.

The three of them were decked out in short dresses that left little to the imagination.

"Where are *you* going?" I asked.

"Out with you," Mandy said.

I glanced down at my yoga pants and T-shirt. "I'm staying home."

"Like hell you are," Mandy said, pushing past Eliza and me and leading the other two inside. "It's been a week. You need to get over that asshole and come out with us."

"I'm over him," I said.

They all scoffed.

"I think we can all agree I've had a shitty start to this school year," I said.

"Are you gonna let that define you?" Melinda asked.

My brows scrunched. "I'm allowed to be upset."

"Of course, you are," Marla said, draping her arm around my shoulders. "But a week is long enough."

"Is it? Because the more photos I see of her at his concerts, the more I want to hurt someone," I said.

"You need to stay off the internet," Eliza said. "It's only hurting you."

I dropped onto the sofa. "I need it to hurt so I can get over him."

"That's not how you get over someone," Marla said.

"It's how I got over Geoffrey."

"Geoffrey was a douchebag," Mandy said. "He made it easy to get over him. Besides, you had a rock—"

"*Mandy*," they chided.

"I just meant you didn't have time to mourn that relationship. This one has been thrown in your face and he never even gave you a reason," she said.

I shrugged. "Silence speaks volumes."

"Then come out with us," Melinda said.

"I'm no fun right now. I know it and you all know it. Take Eliza. Go have fun and let me get over this the only way I know how to."

"By sitting home alone?" Mandy said.

"By sitting home alone," I confirmed.

They left for the bar a little while later, taking Eliza with them. I stayed on the sofa, unable to make the effort to get myself into my room. The impromptu intervention had drained me. They were right. I needed to move on. But they didn't know what being with Kozart had been like. They didn't know how he trusted me with things he trusted no one else with. I thought that made us different. Coming to grips with the fact that it had all been a lie was a difficult pill to swallow. I just needed time.

Kozart

I lay in my hotel bed, the lights off and no sounds except those of the occasional hotel guest or employee walking by my room. I'd gotten my own room, opting to not stay in the penthouse to deal with noise and partying since I was in no mood to party these days. Nor was I in the mood to make nice with the guys. Our shows had been killer and the crowds seemed to be liking the new covers we'd been adding to keep it fresh, but I wasn't myself, probably because I hadn't slept in a week.

I grabbed for my phone and the screen illuminated the pitch-black room. The only unread texts on my screen were from Phoebe. I cleared them.

I'd known Aubrey wouldn't call me. She was too proud to call. Too proud to chase a worthless guy.

But I wasn't about to call her either. I'd asked her to trust me and she hadn't.

Fuuuuuuck.

Things were beginning to blur in my mind.

Was this her fault or mine?

Was she waiting on me to call while I was waiting on her to call me?

Things had become so fucked up. I didn't know which way was up.

One thing I did know for sure. I missed her so damn much. The way her laugh burrowed its way inside me. The way her smile lit up even the darkest space. The way her body fit with mine as if it belonged there.

But I need to get a grip. None of that mattered anymore. I was no better than her cheating ex. And there was no way to convince her otherwise. Nothing would make this whole fucked-up situation right.

I'd told her from the beginning that I wasn't a settle down type of guy. I wished she'd listened. I wished I hadn't given her hope. I wished I hadn't given myself hope.

I closed my eyes and prayed for sleep which I knew would never come.

CHAPTER TWENTY-NINE

Aubrey

I sat in my stuttering class watching a movie about performers who stuttered in their everyday speech, but who could perform without even the slightest hint of a stutter. Of course, my thoughts drifted to Kozart as a boy, being bounced around foster homes while no one got him the help he needed for his stutter. I wondered if singing was the one thing that helped *him* overcome it.

"I need to show you something," Eliza whispered.

My head swung around and my eyes widened at the sight of her in the seat behind me. "What are you doing here?"

"You need to see this," she said, holding her phone so I could see the screen.

I glanced to my professor who was engrossed in the movie then ticked my head toward the back door—the one I assumed she snuck in. "Come on." I slipped out of my seat, with Eliza following behind me. In the empty hallway, I turned to her. "This couldn't wait?"

She held her phone's screen so we could both see it. A video was cued on the screen. "Z's been doing different covers every night."

"I thought you weren't going to listen to his music anymore?" I said, knowing she'd only said that to make me feel better.

"Oh, I—"

I bumped her with my shoulder. "It's fine. You loved Savage Beasts long before Kozart and I...well, you know."

She nodded, not making me have to say it. "People have been posting the new covers because new music is new music. So, last night, he did something completely different and it went viral."

"What do you mean?"

"He sang a country song and it already has over a million views."

My heart accelerated. "He hates country."

"I know. Why do you think I'm here?"

The beating of my pulse filled my ears. I was scared to ask the question, but I needed to know. "What song?"

"'Sleep Without You.'"

My eyes widened. "He sang it in concert?"

She nodded. "The crowd loved his rendition."

"Why would he do that?"

"Listen." She pressed the arrow and the video played.

Kozart sat alone on stage with a single spotlight on him. The crowd sat in darkness screaming at the sight of him.

My heart squeezed in my chest, the whole scene hurting more than I ever imagined it could.

"This is a little unconventional," he said into the single microphone, his eyes bloodshot.

I wondered if he'd been drinking.

Or if he was just tired.

"But I've been working on some new things," he continued. "And playing around with some country songs." The crowd roared. "See if you like it." He broke into "my" song. The same rendition he'd told me was for my ears only. I blinked back stinging tears as he shared my song with the world.

Had *everything* he'd ever said to me been a lie? A big, fat lie that I fell for, hook, line, and sinker?

That knowledge—that truth—was what would make getting over him that much easier now.

CHAPTER THIRTY

Aubrey

My friends and I climbed the stadium steps to our fifty-yard-line section. Our school's football stadium was massive, and this game against Alabama was sold out. The noise rumbled, shaking the pavement beneath my feet. I hadn't been to a game since last year. It seemed like every time we had a home game, I'd been busy with Kozart, missing my normal Saturday ritual with my friends.

"I need a football player," I shouted to my friends as we took our seats.

They all looked to me and danced around, excited by my sudden change in attitude.

We'd tailgated pregame, so my buzz was speaking for me. But I didn't want to disappoint them by admitting it was the liquor talking. Besides, maybe a football player was exactly what I needed.

"Oh, I've got a few who'd die to take you out," Mandy said.

"You've been in a relationship for three years," Melinda added. "Now that you're single, guys are asking about you."

"Seriously?" I said.

"Yes," they all assured me.

I didn't really want another guy. They were nothing but trouble. I was thinking the same thing as we entered the football victory party later that night. The girls had talked me into tiny cutoffs, a tight shirt, and wedges.

"You look so hot," Mandy assured me as we entered the packed living room of some football players' house.

Lots of eyes turned our way as we made our way through the crowd. The stares were either because the triplets received attention everywhere we went, or the people recognized me as the girl who got dumped by the rock star.

As if the attention wasn't annoying enough, Kozart's voice blared through the speakers. Seriously? The universe was definitely toying with me. It just had to be.

The triplets didn't even notice when I left them and walked into the kitchen.

A guy I recognized from my philosophy class manned the keg. He grabbed me a cup and poured me a beer, handing it to me with a smile. "Here you go, beautiful."

"Thanks," I said, tipping back the cup and chugging the contents. Once I finished, I looked to him again. "Can I have another?"

"You bet," he said, grabbing my cup and refilling it.

"Thanks." I took the cup and made my way through the house in search of my friends.

"Aubrey," a voice called from behind me.

I spun around, feeling a little light-headed after downing the beer.

Geoffrey stood there.

Shoot me now.

"Hey." His eyes moved over my outfit. "You look good."

"You look like an asshole. Oh, wait. You are an asshole."

I had to hand it to him. He didn't argue. He just moved closer to me as if I hadn't said anything. "Who you here with?"

"The girls."

"I should've known." He stopped in front of me, lifting his hand and pushing my waves away from my face.

I let him, counting the seconds before my fist connected with his face.

As if he'd heard my thoughts, he dropped his hand.

Wait. Had I said that aloud?

Nope. His hand landed on my hip.

What the hell?

"You wanna go somewhere?" he asked, dropping his voice the way he used to when he was initiating sex.

My brows pinched together. "Somewhere?"

He nodded.

"Where?"

He shrugged. "I don't know. My place?"

Laughter burst out of me. "Are you kidding me?"

He stared straight-faced back at me.

I winced. "Oh, my God, you're serious."

"I just figured, you had enough time to forgive me."

My eyes narrowed.

"And, we're both single now, so—"

"So, you'd take me back to the place we were supposed to live together?"

His eyes averted mine.

"I'm not going anywhere with you tonight…or ever." I spun away from him and walked right out the front door and away from the party.

I slipped off my shoes and carried them as I moved down the dark sidewalk, needing to get as far away as possible from the party and Geoffrey—and Kozart's voice.

I just needed to breathe.

The music became softer the further away from the house I moved. I pulled out my phone and texted Marla as I walked, letting her know I needed to get out of there and would see her and the girls tomorrow.

Maybe it had been too soon to go out.

Raindrops began to fall. Of course, they did. I laughed up to the heavens asking why the last few months of my life had played out the way they had. Their response? A full-blown downpour drenching me to the bone.

I didn't even bother quickening my pace. Since I was barefoot, I didn't need to avoid puddles. I walked right through them. By the time I turned onto my street, I no longer needed a shower. I was water-logged and cold.

My bare feet stopped, my entire body stilling.

A dark car sat parked out front of my condo. Through the driving rain, I couldn't make out the make, but the knots of unease tightening in my stomach told me I knew who it was.

I inhaled deeply and walked the rest of the way, heading up my sidewalk without giving the car a second glance. I made it five steps before I heard a car door slam.

Though my heart began to race, I kept moving, neither slowing nor quickening my pace.

"You're drenched."

Kozart's voice sent a cold shiver up my spine, but I ignored it and kept walking.

"Aubrey."

I reached the door, and my shaking hand struggled to get the key into the lock. *Dammit.*

His feet slapped the puddles as he moved behind me. "Talk to me."

"*Now* you want to talk?" I spun around, my eyes narrowed. "Because I'm not really interested in hearing about your girlfriend."

He huffed, his cargo shorts and black T-shirt just as drenched as my clothes. "She's not my girlfriend."

Drunken, angry laughter shot out of me. "Oh, you really think I'm dense, don't you?" I continued to laugh as I wiped the rain off my face. "I'll admit, I *was* in the beginning. But not now."

He stepped toward me.

"Stay back," I said through clenched teeth.

He winced at my harsh tone.

I turned back to my door, still struggling with the damn key.

"I fucked everything up. And I have no idea how to fix it."

"There's no fixing it. You made me a promise which you didn't keep."

He growled. "You promised me that you trusted me."

I spun back toward him, surprising even myself. "Do *not* put this on me."

He dug his hands into his pockets.

"Did *she* help you sleep?"

His face scrunched. "What? No."

I rolled my eyes, unable to believe anything that came out of his mouth anymore. "You showing up like this isn't fair, Kozart. Just leave me alone." I turned back to the door. This time my key twisted in the lock and I was able to open it.

"I thought you'd fight for me."

I gasped, his words a kick to my gut.

Had he gone and lost his freaking mind?

"I thought you would've believed me and not what you thought you saw. When you didn't, I knew you never really trusted me."

My fingers clenched at my sides. Who the hell did he think he was? Radio silence and then he wanted *me* to fight for *him*? I could barely control my emotions. I spun back around. "Why would I fight for someone who doesn't want me?"

"I never said I didn't want you."

"You never *said* anything. *Remember*?"

His eyes flashed down.

My arms flew out to my sides. "Do you think I'm blind? I *saw* you at the hotel with *her*."

"What did you really see?"

I jerked a glance over my shoulder as if he was talking to someone inside the open door. He was talking so crazy right now he could *not* have been talking to me. I looked back to him in disbelief. "Are you on something?"

"I'm serious, Aubrey. What did you see? You saw some actress walk into a hotel with me."

"Yes, Kozart. I saw some actress walk into a hotel with *my* man."

His teeth clamped together and his jaw ticked.

"What more did I need to see? The two of you going at it in an elevator? Or better yet, the two of you naked in your shower?"

He said nothing, though the red creeping up his neck into his cheeks told me I'd hit a nerve.

Good. He deserved my honesty.

"It's not how it looks."

I scoffed. "Of course it is."

He scrubbed both hands up and down his wet face. "I thought you knew me. I thought you trusted me. I thought you'd fucking fight for me."

"Now I know you've lost it. *You* stopped calling *me*."

"No one has ever fought for me, Aubrey," he said, as if he'd missed my last comment. "I thought if anyone would, *you* would."

Bile crept up the back of my throat. I would *not* feel sorry for him. I would *not* feel sorry for the guy who broke my heart. "You sang my song. You said it was for my ears only then you sang it for the world."

"So, *you'd* hear it," he countered. "So, you'd come back to me."

I rolled my eyes and shook my head.

"None of it's how it seems, Aubrey. Don't you get it?" he said. "My team needed me to be connected to someone who wasn't in college. They needed to get rid of the notion that I was dating college girls. It looked bad for me which looked bad for them."

My eyes narrowed. "You can't actually believe that."

"It doesn't matter what I believe."

Was that the truth? Was that really what happened? *Stop falling for everything he says, Aubrey.*

"I should've been honest with you as soon as I found out what they had planned with Phoebe," he continued. "I should've warned you. But I think, deep down, I needed to see if you really cared about me and trusted me the way I did you. I know it's fucked up, but I wanted to know if you thought I was worth fighting for. Before the band, nobody ever thought I was worth anything, Aubrey. That notion fucks with your head. It stays in the back of your mind."

"I wasn't gonna fight for you if you moved on."

Pained by my words, he closed his eyes and nodded. "I get that now. That's why I'm here. I need you more than I need you to fight for me. I just want you back."

All of this information, mixed with the fact that I'd been drinking all day and was now standing in the pouring rain, swirled through my head haphazardly. My emotions couldn't be trusted. "It's too late. You broke my heart, Kozart. I always knew you would."

"They gave me an ultimatum," he argued.

"And as soon as things got tough, you didn't choose me. You chose *you*."

His eyes lowered to the ground.

That told me all I needed to know. "Goodbye, Kozart." I turned and walked inside, closing the door behind me.

Once I climbed the steps and reached my condo, Eliza opened the door. "Are you okay?" she asked, probably witnessing the whole scene from the window.

"I'm soaking wet and Kozart just showed up to see me. No. I'm not okay."

I stripped out of my wet clothes as I walked down the hall, tossing them into the laundry basket in my room.

"What'd he say?" Eliza asked, dropping down onto my bed.

I turned my back to her as I took off my bra and slipped a T-shirt over my head. "Nothing that made it better."

"But he showed up."

"And only disappointed me."

"I'm sorry," she said.

Not half as sorry as I was for believing Kozart Savage could ever really love me the way I deserved to be loved.

CHAPTER THIRTY-ONE

Aubrey

I'd been studying in the library for hours, trying to give myself a change of scenery. But nothing erased the images of Kozart in the rain. The words he'd uttered. The pain in his eyes. I closed my laptop and lowered my head onto the table, exhausted and confused.

If dating the actress *was* just for show, and he really wanted me back, wouldn't I just be setting myself up for more heartache? Because he would break my heart. Maybe not purposely, but it was inevitable.

That wouldn't be a relationship. It would be a bull ride, where I'd constantly be hanging on by a thread.

And could I really trust him?

Between him and Geoffrey, they'd left me little confidence in men.

If I learned one thing from Geoffrey, it was that love wasn't supposed to hurt. And with Kozart, all the outside factors at play—all the unknowing—would continue to hurt me.

My phone vibrated next to me.

I lifted my head and grabbed it, expecting it to be a text from Eliza checking on me.

But it wasn't from Eliza.

It was from Kozart. **Obviously, I'm no good with words.**

I sucked in a breath as another text appeared.

I need to make this better.

A link popped up. A playlist. Then another text.

Please just listen. These songs say it all.

I closed my eyes, willing myself not to pull my earbuds from my bag. I didn't need to hear anything to know we were over. To know we could never work. Why was he doing this to me? Couldn't he just leave me alone?

I stared at the link.

My eyes flicked to my messenger bag where my earbuds sat in the inside pocket.

I looked back to the link.

Dammit.

I pulled my earbuds out of my bag and tucked them into my ears.

I paused. I didn't need to do this. I didn't.

Who was I kidding?

I clicked on the link and the rock song, "Perfect" by Hedley played. I'd heard it before, but now I found myself concentrating on the lyrics. Concentrating on why Kozart included it, first no less. The singer claimed not to be perfect. Claimed that the relationship couldn't be over. Claimed to be trying since that's what he promised to do from the beginning.

Gavin DeGraw's "Stay" played next. I'd never heard it before so I really listened to the words. He sang of needing another chance and not wanting the girl to walk away because he needed her. *Huh.* If only Kozart had realized that before. The song continued and the lyrics about finding "the one" made me wonder if he actually viewed me that way.

I wouldn't have thought Kozart knew any country songs—other than the ones I included in his playlist, but the next song was Morgan Wallen's "Whiskey Glasses." I guess I didn't need to wonder what he'd been doing lately. I'd seen his bloodshot eyes in the video. And while

I knew he selected these songs for a reason, I wouldn't feel bad that he had regrets now and was drowning those regrets in alcohol.

"All We'd Ever Need," by Lady Antebellum followed. And if that wasn't a tearjerker, I didn't know what was. I wondered if he truly was feeling like me. And if he knew I'd been sleeping in his T-shirt.

"Wanted" by Hunter Hayes played next. I wish Kozart wanted me to feel wanted when I was standing outside the hotel with his gift in my hand.

Of course, Kozart included Brett Young's "Sleep Without You," as well as "In Case You Didn't Know." The title summed up the song, and I tried not to read too much into the fact that he sang about how much he loved the girl. Is that what Kozart was trying to say to me? Did he love me?

"Speechless" by Dan and Shay, one of my all-time favorite songs, drifted through the earbuds next. The singer is so in love with his soon-to-be-bride. The song is every girl's dream song because who wouldn't want a song sung about how beautiful they are and how speechless they made their man?

The last song was Jason Aldean's, "You Make It Easy." I found it ironic. If I made it easy, why had Kozart gone and made it so difficult?

The playlist ended, and I sat alone in the dim library.

I had to hand it to him. He'd chosen songs he normally wouldn't have listened to. Had he been listening to my music while we'd been apart? The songs definitely painted a vivid picture. But had I interpreted everything correctly?

And did he really think a playlist would make everything better?

CHAPTER THIRTY-TWO

Aubrey

"You've got to be kidding me, Caroline," I said to my sister over my car's speaker as I drove toward my parents' house.

"I'm sorry," she said.

"If I knew, I could've gone home with the triplets," I said.

"I know. If I knew he was coming, I wouldn't have allowed it."

"I can't believe Mom and Dad did."

"They're not happy about it either. They just thought it'd be Rick's parents," she said. "When will you be here?"

"When I get there," I said before disconnecting the call.

I spotted the nearest exit and took it, needing to stop to gather my wits. I knew today was going to be tough, given the fact that I'd have to field questions about what happened with Kozart and me. But now that we were going to be hosting unexpected guests, everything would be a mess.

I pulled into a café parking lot, noting the single car parked there. It made sense. Everyone else was home with their families. Too bad my parents' house was now the last place I wanted to be.

I stepped out of my car, tugging down the hem of my fitted green dress as I walked to the entrance, needing a coffee—and wanting to waste as much time as humanly possible.

I grabbed my coffee and slipped into a corner seat.

This sucked.

Alone in a café on Thanksgiving. Avoiding my parents and the unexpected guests who'd ruin my day.

I scanned the newsfeed on my phone. The triplets and their family appeared in numerous posts. I laughed to myself, missing those crazy girls and wishing I'd gone home with them.

A texted appeared on my screen. **Where are you?**

I didn't respond to Caroline's text, but knew hiding out in a café would not make the inevitable day disappear. But it would make it shorter.

A half hour later, I parked in the road in front of my parents' house—since the driveway was already filled with cars.

I sucked in a deep breath and stepped out of the car, carrying the bottle of wine I'd brought. As I neared the door, I heard the chatter of everyone inside and my stomach turned.

Smile, Aubrey. Smile.

I pulled open my parents' side door and stepped into the kitchen. Voices lowered once they spotted me. I smiled at my sister and her new husband Rick. They looked scared.

My mom rushed over, throwing her arms around me and whispering in my ear. "I love you. I'm sorry. I couldn't say no when I heard her sister got sick and they had nowhere to go. But I had no idea *he* was coming."

"I'm fine," I said as she released me and I handed her the wine.

My dad hugged me. "I'll kill him if he even looks at you."

"I'm good," I assured him, stifling a smile.

When he stepped away, my sister handed me a big glass of wine. "Here. You're gonna need this."

I took it, gulping down half the glass like the lush I needed to be to get through this hellish day. I walked down the hall to the living room. Geoffrey sat beside his dad on the sofa and his mom sat across the room in a wing-backed chair. "Hello," I said from the doorway.

Geoffrey's mom jumped up, throwing her arms around me. "Sweetheart." She pulled back to look at me. "Look how beautiful you look. Have you lost weight? Look how skinny you are." She looked to her husband, who'd stood from the sofa. "Jim, look how beautiful Aubrey looks."

"Hi, honey," he said, hugging me.

"Hi, Jim," I said, feeling beyond awkward. These people could have been my future in-laws had their son not cheated on me.

I looked to Geoffrey with raised brows as if to say, *What the hell?*

He stood. I took a step back. "Happy Thanksgiving, Aubs." Knowing I wouldn't cause a scene in front of his parents, he outstretched his arms. I stood there with my arms down at my sides as he wrapped his arms around me.

"I sense sparks flying again," his mom said to her husband.

"I've been texting you," Geoffrey whispered into my ear.

"I blocked your number," I whispered back.

As if on cue, my mom called from the kitchen, "Let's eat."

I spun away from Geoffrey and made my way to the dining room, gulping the rest of my wine as I walked. I sat at the end of the table beside the head, grasping my sister's hand and pulling her down into the seat beside me as my dad sat at the head. That left my mom across from me. Jim took the other head and Geoffrey and his mom sat on either side of him. *Phew.*

Caroline poured me another glass of wine, knowing it would take a lot more of it to get through this day. Playing nice with Geoffrey, and being reminded that this would've been my life if he and I ended up together, overwhelmed me.

"This looks lovely," Geoffrey's mother gushed over the spread my mother put out. "We so appreciate you having us so last minute."

My mother smiled, her southern hospitality shining through. "We're pleased to have you."

The food was passed around until all our plates had been filled. Then my dad led us in saying grace.

"A tradition in our house is to go around and say what we're thankful for," he told Geoffrey's parents. "Caroline, why don't you start."

My sister smiled. "I'm thankful for my new husband and all our future plans."

Everyone smiled at her newly-wedded bliss.

"Rick," my dad prompted.

"I'm grateful for my new bride and the family I inherited with her." He glanced to me and flashed me a sincere smile. "And I'm also thankful that my parents were able to join us, albeit unexpectedly." Again, he glanced to me, this time regrettably.

His parents were grateful for all of us and the food.

"Geoffrey?" my dad said, trying to say his name without jumping across the table and stabbing him in the eye like he would've liked to.

"I'm thankful that I get to spend the holiday with Aubrey." He looked to me with hopeful eyes.

I have no idea how I didn't stick my finger down my throat and gag.

"I never thought I'd have the chance to again," he added.

"It wasn't my choice." I tipped back my wine and finished it off. "And if we're all being honest here, I'd just like to make it clear that Geoffrey and I are never getting back together."

Geoffrey's eyes narrowed on mine, angry and likely embarrassed that I'd done it at the table in front of everyone.

"That ship has sailed," I continued, unable to stop myself. "Actually, it hit an iceberg and sank."

Caroline snorted.

"Aubrey?" my dad said, likely amused but trying to rein me in. "You didn't say what you're grateful for."

I poured myself a full glass of wine, having no idea what I was thankful for. This whole meal was such a sham. "I'm thankful for…rainbows and fireflies."

My parents laughed nervously.

"I'm thankful for having all of you here today," my mom quickly added, stopping me from continuing.

"And I'm thankful for having my three girls all under one roof for the day," my dad concluded. "Let's eat."

We dug into the food. Geoffrey's parents made small talk with my parents and Caroline and Rick. I caught Geoffrey staring at me multiple times, but I dodged his eye contact, staring at the mound of mashed potatoes on my plate that I knew I wouldn't eat.

"So, Aubrey," Geoffrey's mom began. "Caroline mentioned you were dating that famous musician."

A lump shot to my throat as forks clinked on dishes. I should've known this was coming after I'd rejected her baby.

"But then I saw that he's dating that movie star Phoebe Larsen," Geoffrey's mother continued.

"No, he's not," a deep voice said.

My eyes widened as everyone turned toward the voice.

Kozart stood in the doorway in dark jeans and a light blue collared shirt holding a bouquet of flowers. "I knocked."

"What are you doing here?" I asked, the words slipping out before I could stop them.

"You invited m-me," he said. "Remember?"

My pulse began to pound in my temples.

This was not happening. This was *not* happening.

"Aubrey, why don't you grab your guest a chair," my mother suggested.

I pushed my chair back, scraping it along the floor as I stood, having no intention of getting Kozart a chair. I glanced to my sister and Geoffrey whose eyes were fixed on Kozart. Geoffrey glowering and my sister about ready to fall off her chair. I shook my head and stormed into the kitchen.

I heard Kozart in the dining room. "These are for you." I assumed he handed my mother the bouquet. "Thanks for having m-me."

I stood against the kitchen counter with my arms crossed, trying to regulate my staggered breathing. What the hell was he doing here? Yes, I'd invited him. But that was before. *Way* before and he knew it.

He stepped slowly into the kitchen, obviously treading lightly.

I stared at him, unable to accept that he was standing in my parents' kitchen. Unable to comprehend why he thought it was a good idea. "Why are you here?"

"Why do you th-think?" he stuttered.

I shrugged. "Your supermodel was busy?"

"Stop."

"Go."

He stepped forward. "Can we go somewhere and ta-talk?"

"We're talking right now."

"Cut me some sl-lack, Aubrey," he stuttered again, his eyes averting mine as he cursed under his breath.

I sucked in a breath. Oh my God. He was *stuttering*. My mind reeled, flashing back to what he'd told me when we met. He stuttered when he was extremely nervous. *Shit*. My chest tightened around my heart and tears pricked at my eyes. "Fine," I said, walking toward the side door while trying to stop the tears welling in my eyes. I stepped outside and Kozart followed me.

I didn't know where to go, so I walked to the end of the driveway and followed the sidewalk along my parents' road.

Kozart kept pace with me. "I'm sorry you didn't expect m-me."

I shrugged.

"Are you back with your ex?"

I avoided his gaze. "What do you care?"

"Of course, I c-care."

"I'm not back with him. I just found out he and his parents were gonna be here on my way over. I almost turned around and went back to campus."

"You would've b-been alone."

I shrugged, trying to ignore his stutter, but it was slowly breaking my already broken heart. "Beats the alternative."

We walked in silence for a long time.

"Why are you really here?" I finally said.

"Did you get my pl-playlist?"

I nodded.

"I miss y-you."

My heart squeezed in my chest, both loving and hating his words.

He stopped walking and grabbed my hand, stopping me mid-step.

As much as I wanted to shake him off, I let him hold on, missing the contact more than I wanted to admit. Did that make me weak? Did it make me compassionate? Who the hell knew.

"I miss you so damn m-much," he continued.

I pulled in a deep breath and exhaled it slowly, having no idea what to say. I just needed his stuttering to stop. And my pain to stop. And—

"You are the best thing that's ever happened to me, Aubrey, and I pushed you away. And for w-what? To be alone and m-miserable? Because these past weeks have been hell for me. Complete h-hell."

I said nothing, but tears filled my eyes. I closed them, hoping it would stop the tears, but they escaped, trailing down my cheeks. I opened my eyes, knowing I couldn't disguise them.

Kozart dropped my hand and reached up, catching my tears with his thumbs. "The fact that you're cr-crying, makes me think that I'm not the only one who's been mi-miserable."

I said nothing.

"I know I hurt you. I know I fucked up big t-time. But I want to prove to you that I'm not that g-guy."

"As far as I know, you're still with that actress."

He cocked his head. "I'm not. I never was."

"See? That's the thing. Your word means nothing to me right now."

He huffed his frustration.

"And, what about your team? They want you with a celebrity."

"I don't give a f-fuck what they want," he said. "I know what I want. And I just want us to be okay again."

"We can't be okay. Not after everything that happened."

"I don't believe th-that," he said.

We circled back to my parents' house. I noticed Arthur parked out front. Had he been there before? "Doesn't Arthur have family to spend Thanksgiving with?"

He shook his head.

"Let me run in and make him a plate of food you can take with you," I said.

"Does that mean I don't get to stay?"

"I think it's better if you don't."

He nodded regrettably. "But don't take me leaving as me giving up."

Did that make me happy?

I was definitely happy his stutter seemed to be subsiding. It was difficult to be angry with him when he was stuttering like the scared child he once was.

He followed me inside the kitchen. Luckily, only my mom and sister were in there cleaning the dishes.

"I'm just gonna make a dish for Kozart's driver," I said to them.

"Oh, why don't you invite your driver in," my mom said to him.

His eyes cut to mine.

"They have to head out," I explained.

My mom grabbed some plastic containers and began filling them for me. "Would you like one, too?" she asked Kozart.

"That would be great," he said.

I glanced to my sister who gaped at Kozart. I rolled my eyes. "Caroline. Have you met Kozart?"

The transformation from speechless fan to composed sister happened before my eyes. "Just at my wedding," she said, reaching out her hand to shake his.

He pulled her into a hug and whispered something into her ear that made her giggle.

Damn rock star charm.

When he pulled away, her eyes were wide and dazed.

My mom put the filled plastic containers into a bag and handed it to Kozart. "I'm sorry you can't stay. I would've liked to learn more about you."

He glanced to me before looking back to her. "Yeah. Maybe next time I'm in town Aubrey will bring me over with her."

My stomach clenched as I walked to the door, urging him to follow me.

"Good night," he said to them before following me outside.

The sun had already set, so the single light beside the side door was the only light in the driveway. We walked side by side down to the car. I pulled open the front passenger door, catching Arthur off guard. "Happy Thanksgiving, Arthur. My mom packed you a meal."

He smiled. "Thank you, Aubrey. I'm sure it'll be wonderful."

"Good night," I said before closing the door and turning to Kozart who stood staring at his shoes. "So…I guess this is good night."

His eyes lifted slowly. "I'm gonna prove you can trust me again." He pulled open the back door and began to climb in the back seat. He stopped and looked back at me. He never looked back. "I won't lose you twice." He didn't wait for a response, climbing into the back seat and closing himself inside.

Caroline appeared beside me as the car pulled away from the sidewalk. "You okay?"

"I have no idea," I said, watching the car disappear around the corner.

"I think it will all work out," she said. "I saw the way he looked at you."

"He's a rock star. He's got the smoldering look down."

She laughed. "Yeah, he definitely has it down."

"I can't believe he showed up."

"Didn't you invite him?" she asked.

"When we were together."

"Showing up now took nerve."

I nodded, knowing it had taken nerve for him to show up at my parents' house. More nerve than I would've thought.

"You know, Aubs. He could have any girl on this planet, and he chose you."

"He didn't though. That's the reason we're not together."

"But he obviously realizes his mistake. He came here for *you*."

I knew he did. And I knew he said he wanted me back. But what happened when he changed his mind? Or his team gave him another ultimatum? Where would that leave me?

"He said he's gonna win you back," Caroline said.

My eyes cut to hers.

"That's what he whispered in my ear. That failure's not an option."

CHAPTER THIRTY-THREE

Aubrey

"You're never gonna believe this," Eliza said as she swept through the front door of our condo Sunday night and dropped her suitcase on the floor.

I sat on the sofa, having just unpacked my clothes from the long weekend. "Welcome back to you, too."

"He's here."

"Who's here?"

"Z."

I sat up, my eyes sweeping the living room. "What do you mean?"

"Just get a sweatshirt on and come with me."

"Where are we going?"

"You just need to come with me."

Five minutes later I was in my white hoodie and jeans, speed-walking toward campus with Eliza leading the way like a bat out of hell. For a Sunday night after a holiday, there were tons of people around, many of them rushing in the same direction as us.

As we neared campus, the soft hum of music greeted us. The closer we got, the louder the music became. "Tell me he's not…"

"Oh, he definitely is and if you don't walk faster, we're gonna miss all their best songs."

"His whole band's here?"

She nodded, the excitement in her eyes a stark contrast to the fear in mine.

A huge stage with lights flashing down on it sat in the quad. Hundreds of people stood in front of the stage moving to the rock music now blasting through the speakers.

Kozart stood at center stage with one foot on one of the smaller speakers in front of him. He sang "Midnight."

Eliza led us to the left side of the stage, off to the side so we didn't get pinned between bodies pushing toward the front.

Reggie stood by the side of the stage. His eyes were on mine. He nodded once, as if that small gesture erased what happened between us. Thinking back, I liked to believe he was just looking out for me and trying to spare my feelings.

"This next song is for someone very special to me," Kozart said.

My attention shifted to him.

"She's one of your own." His eyes purposefully searched the crowd. "And I'm hoping she heard about our little impromptu concert like all of you did."

The crowd grew louder.

"She's someone I trust implicitly but who needs to learn to trust me again." He wiped a towel across his sweaty face. "She's someone who gives me those fucked up butterflies every time she enters a room."

The girls in the crowd screamed, probably stunned this tough rock star admitted to getting butterflies.

Wait. *I* give *him* butterflies?

"You may know this country hit," he continued. "If you do, sing along." He broke into "Speechless," by Dan and Shay, though a grittier rock version.

"You lucky bitch," Eliza said.

I scoffed. I didn't feel lucky over the past month. I felt like my heart had been ripped out of my chest and trampled on by a herd of angry animals.

I glanced around at the growing crowd. Cell phones were raised in the air as he sang a song so different from his heavy rock songs. But apparently, he could do no wrong because the crowd sang along.

After singing "Speechless," he sang all their biggest hits, to the obvious delight of everyone there.

"Good night, Tennessee!" he called to the screaming fans a little while later. "Thanks for being here!"

Once the music ended and the lights switched off, everyone turned, heading back to wherever they'd come from when they discovered Savage Beasts was performing a free concert.

"Hey," Eliza said to me. "The big oaf is waving at you."

I glanced to Reggie who was beckoning me over.

Eliza dragged me to the side of the stage with her.

Reggie stepped to the side, indicating a small area to pass through to the backstage area. "He wants to see you."

"He knows where I live," I said, turning away from Reggie and taking off for home.

"What the hell did you just do?" Eliza asked, hurrying after me.

"He said he planned to prove that he wanted me back."

"He just held a free concert for you. That's not proof?"

I shrugged.

She laughed, though more out of surprise than amusement.

Once we returned to our condo, Eliza ducked into her room—giving me privacy in case he showed up. I dropped onto the sofa. Kozart and I needed to talk. We didn't need a repeat of the last time he showed up in my bedroom.

And, how did I feel about him showing up? Arranging a free concert on my campus? Telling everyone I gave him butterflies?

Most would be elated. And while I wouldn't lie and say I wasn't taken aback by his grand gestures, I was still hesitant. He'd broken my heart after assuring me he wouldn't.

There was a knock on my door. A shiver rushed through me. Was I ready to see him? Could I remain strong with him in front of me?

I pushed myself to my feet and moved to the door. A wave of emotions echoed through me as I tugged it open.

Kozart stood there, his lips twitching in the corners.

"Nice show," I said.

"I did it for you," he said, his eyes absorbing the details of my face as if he hadn't seen me in years. "Any chance you're gonna let me in?"

I stepped to the side, and he brushed by me, his just-showered scent taunting me with familiarity as it drifted around me. He circled the living room, clearly waiting for me to tell him to sit.

"Have a seat."

He sat on the arm of the sofa, not committing to a real seat.

I leaned my hip against the chair. "So…"

He chuckled, knowing I said that when I had something to say but didn't know how to say it. "So."

"Where you heading next?"

234 | J . N a t h a n

"I've got some time off between now and Christmas," he said.

"Oh…I bet your band loved having to show up here to perform. Don't they want to get home?"

He shrugged. "They owed me."

"For what?"

He got quiet. "The whole ultimatum thing. They didn't have my back."

A heavy silence descended.

Had his friends really forced him to choose? Had he really been in a no-win situation?

"Tell me you're happy to see me," he said.

I crossed my arms, too stubborn to respond.

He stood, moving slowly toward me.

I sucked in a breath.

"I want to be with you, Aubrey. Just you," he said, the sincerity in his eyes clear as he hovered over me.

I stared back at him, appreciating his words and wishing his scent wasn't working its way into my senses.

"Nothing?"

"Did you expect to show up here and everything be back to normal?" I asked.

"I didn't expect it. I hoped for it, though."

"Don't you know me at all?" I asked.

"Yes. That's what I've been trying to tell you. I know you and you know me."

"That doesn't erase what happened. I knew you before you screwed me over."

I watched my words hit him like a blow.

"I'm not trying to hurt you, Kozart. I'm just trying to be honest."

He nodded his understanding. "I hurt you. You're just guarding your heart."

"I'd be a fool not to."

"You're not a fool," he said.

Feeling vulnerable under his gaze, I avoided his eyes.

"Can I stay a while? Just sit with you and watch TV or something?" he asked.

I thought about all the reasons it was a terrible idea. All the reasons I needed to be careful. All the reasons I was incapable of saying no to him. With a deep exhalation, I relented. "When I say it's time to go, you need to go."

"Absolutely." He slipped down onto the sofa and touched the empty spot beside him.

I sat down in the chair across the room.

He cocked his head. "I'm not gonna try anything if you sit next to me."

I stared at him, that pull we once had still existing— even as I fought to resist it. I stood slowly and sat down beside him, making sure no part of my body touched his.

"That's better," he said. "Did you like the song?"

"I love that song."

"But did you love it when I sang it?"

I shrugged. "It was different."

"Stop being so tough."

"What do you want from me?"

He turned to look at me, his eyes boring into mine. "I want to see you smile again. But I know I'm the reason you're not smiling, and it sucks. Just tell me what I need to do."

We stared at each other, both knowing I wanted to forgive him. And he wanted me to forgive him. But my brain and heart were battling. And I couldn't make them stop.

"Come here," he said, stretching his arm out across the back of the sofa.

I paused for a long moment, knowing my resolve was weakening. I moved an inch closer. His hand dropped onto my shoulder and he pulled me closer, tucking me into his side. Tears stung my eyes as we sat there, not together, but not enemies either. "This is weird," I said.

"No, this is a start."

I said nothing, probably because I had no idea what to say.

"Thanks for sending the meals with me and Arthur," he said. "I haven't had home cooking like that in…well probably ever."

I nodded, understanding why he'd never had them.

"I really wanted to stay."

I nodded again, knowing he did.

"I really wanted to knock out your ex in the middle of dessert."

Laughter burst out of me.

He chuckled too. "I hate him."

"Not as much as I do."

"That dinner had to suck."

"Especially when we had to say what we were thankful for," I said.

"What'd you say?"

I shrugged. "Something about rainbows and fireflies."

"Isn't it rainbows and butterflies?" he asked.

"Well, I like fireflies."

"I'll have to remember that. And for the record, I would've said I was thankful for you."

"*Riiight.*"

"I'm serious. I would've said I'm thankful that you came into my life after some asshole lost you."

I laughed again. "Yeah, that would've gone over well with Geoffrey and his parents at the table."

"I can take them."

"I don't doubt it."

I don't know how it happened. It might've been the warmth of his body. Or the ease of our conversation. Or the comfort I felt in his arms. But my eyelids fluttered shut and sleep pulled me under.

CHAPTER THIRTY-FOUR

Aubrey

Sunshine filled my living room as I stretched out my sore neck, a side effect of the sitting position I'd fallen asleep in beside Kozart. Soft purrs escaped him. I took the moment to stare at him. The stubble on his jaw line. His rosy cheeks due to my body being pressed to his all night. His long eyelashes fanned out over the tops of his cheeks.

"Stop staring at me," his raspy morning voice said.

"I was just noticing the drool on the side of your mouth."

His hand flew up, wiping away at his mouth. "There's no drool." His eyes fluttered open. "I slept like a rock. I haven't slept like that since…well you know."

"Actually, I don't."

He huffed. "I swear to you, nothing happened with Phoebe. It was all for show. I admit, she didn't necessarily know that. But that's all it ever was for me. She probably thought I was gay since I didn't try anything on her, but you know why I didn't."

I did know. And I did like hearing that nothing happened.

He'd kept his promise to me, even if I didn't know it at the time.

"None of this is your fault, Aubrey. I take full responsibility."

Eliza stepped out of her room yawning and stretching in her old robe, her unruly bed-head prominent.

"Hey, Eliza," Kozart said, knowing exactly what he was doing.

Her eyes splayed when she noticed him beside me on the sofa. "Oh. Hi." She spun around and hurried back to her room, slamming the door behind her.

I chuckled, amused by how tongue-tied he made her.

"Now, if only I had that effect on you," he said.

I went to push myself up, but he grabbed my arm and pulled me back down, wrapping his arms around me. "Thank you for letting me stay." His arms quickly slipped away, probably not wanting to push me too far.

Sadly, I missed the feel of him. Missed the way everything had always just felt so right and been so easy when we were together.

I grabbed my phone from the end table and checked the time. "I've got class in an hour."

"Can I walk you?"

My head retracted. "Walk me?"

"Yup. Just like a normal couple would do. Walk to class together."

I swallowed down my surprise. "People will see."

"So what?"

"Isn't that what got us into this situation in the first place?"

He ignored my question. "What class do you have?"

"Stuttering. Actually, we watched a film about performers who stutter but not when they're performing."

"Yeah, I've heard of that. You think your professor would let me sit in?"

I tipped my head to the side. "Are you gonna add to the discussion or just distract all the girls in the class?"

He chuckled. "Probably both."

Half an hour later, we walked out of my condo. Kozart took my bag from me and crossed the strap across his chest.

"You don't have to carry that."

"I want to." He reached over and linked our fingers.

My eyes shot down to our conjoined hands.

"Too soon?" he asked.

I shrugged.

"Well, you're not digging your fingernails into my hand, so I'd say that's a good sign."

I stifled a smile and led us toward campus. Monday mornings were always busy, with students rushing in all directions. On campus, heads turned, many doing double-takes. Kozart seemed oblivious to the attention—or he was just so used to it that he ignored it. "People might snap photos."

"So, let them."

"Who are you?" I asked.

We eventually arrived at my stuttering class. Audible gasps filled the room as I approached the professor, with Kozart on my heels. "Professor Blake. Would you mind if my…"

"Her boyfriend," Kozart interrupted.

My eyes cut to his, unsure if I appreciated the save or hated him for it. I looked to the professor. "He'd like to sit in on the class. He had stuttering issues as a child."

"Of course," Professor Blake said, clearly recognizing Kozart. "But I'm going to need an autograph for my wife before you leave."

"You bet," Kozart said with his signature smirk before following me to my seat.

The whispers that ensued were comical, especially from the girls who'd laughed at me when we weren't together. Speaking of which…

"Hey girls," I said approaching them before sitting.

They all stared at Kozart, speechless. I understood their reactions. Having him in front of you was intimidating, and the fact that I was purposely shoving it in their faces, had their tails between their legs.

"I lied when I said Z and I weren't together. I'm sorry I couldn't be honest with you." I shrugged. "I guess it comes with the territory when you date someone in the public eye."

Kozart, catching on that I was purposely rubbing it in their faces, draped his arm over my shoulders. "Hey ladies."

They all mumbled something, flushing beyond reason.

"We can sit down now," I said to him before leading us to two seats in the back of the classroom.

My professor acknowledged Kozart in the back of the room at the start of class—though most of the class' attention had been on him since he entered. "So, you've all noticed our guest today."

People laughed.

"But I'm told that the subject of our class hits close to home for him."

The laughter in the room subsided.

"Would you mind sharing your experience?" he asked Kozart.

Everyone turned to Kozart and I worried this might put him in an uncomfortable situation—one that could bring about his stuttering. "Sure."

I released a nervous breath.

"I stuttered from an early age. I'm not really sure when it started, but I can't remember a time when I didn't stutter."

I watched as Kozart monopolized the discussion in a good way. He was eloquent and honest, not an easy feat in a room full of strangers.

"As a kid, I had no idea how to make the stuttering stop, so I found myself keeping quiet instead of embarrassing myself by speaking. People probably thought I was mute."

A few people laughed, though he wasn't trying to be funny. I felt my body tensing at the thought of him not talking for fear of being made fun of. As if he didn't have enough troubles as a kid.

"Then, I reached high school and realized I could sing," he continued. "Singing made my stutter disappear. So, I knew if it disappeared then, there was a way to remove it from my every day speech. The more I sang, the less prevalent my stutter became until it ultimately disappeared."

"So, you never saw a speech pathologist?" my professor asked.

Kozart shook his head. "But from what Aubrey tells me, they could've given me techniques and strategies to overcome it."

"Yes. Fairly easy strategies, too," my professor explained.

"Well, it's good to know that people like Aubrey will be taking care of the kids today who struggle like I did." His eyes cut to mine and I couldn't help but smile at the brave man beside me.

* * *

After class, Kozart offered to take me to lunch. I knew taking him into a campus restaurant would've drawn too much attention and unnecessary company, so we grabbed takeout from a small café and walked back to my condo.

A shoebox-sized box sat outside my front door.

"Oh," Kozart said when he saw the box.

"Do you know what it is?" I asked as I checked the label which was addressed to me.

"You can open it inside." He picked it up and carried it inside my condo, placing it on the coffee table.

"Did you send it?"

He nodded. "But I had no idea it would come while I was here."

My brows inverted. "Do you want me to wait to open it?"

He shook his head as he dropped down onto the sofa and rested his elbows on his thighs. His hands wringing in front of him unnerved me.

I grabbed a knife from the kitchen then sat beside him, slipping the blade under the tape on the box. Once the flaps were separated, I reached inside and pulled out a much smaller box. I glanced to Kozart.

His eyes looked vulnerable and he seemed nervous. "Open it."

I pulled off the top of the box.

My heart leaped to my throat.

A necklace with a half heart charm sat inside.

"You hold some of my firsts," he said, reaching in the front of his T-shirt and pulling out his own chain with the other half of the heart on it. "I wanted to be able to give you something no one else has."

I couldn't take much more of us being in limbo. Everything about him being there, everything about his words and actions, told me I needed to end this standoff.

"You have my heart, Aubrey. And I don't want it back."

I closed my eyes, knowing I was done. Tears glazed them when I opened them again.

"Aw, babe. I didn't want to make you cry."

I cocked my head as I placed the box back down on the coffee table.

"I'm serious. I just wanted to show you I was listening. And show you I wanna give you everything you've ever wanted."

Surrendering, I climbed into his lap, wrapping my arms around him and holding on tightly. His whole body relaxed in my embrace. His hands drifted up my back and held onto me as I held onto him. I breathed him in. He was doing the same. It had been so long since I felt at home.

He pulled back, his hands lifting to my cheeks, his fingertips drifting over my skin. "You got me a skateboard."

"I did."

"It's the best gift I've ever gotten," he said. "Please tell me you forgive me."

I stared into his blue eyes. They no longer felt unfamiliar. They felt like portals to his soul. A soul that regretted his actions. A soul that was one with mine. A soul I couldn't stay away from any longer. I nodded.

His smile stretched across his face. He said nothing, just leaned into me and kissed me. Elation rushed through me as his lips devoured mine. His tongue pushed its way inside my mouth as I held onto him, loving his eagerness and excitement.

He stood, with me clutched to him, my ankles linking behind his back. He carried me down the hall into my room, his mouth never leaving mine. He lowered me down onto my bed, and only then did he desert my mouth. "We don't have to."

"Yes, we do," I said.

He chuckled as he reached behind his head and pulled off his shirt. His chain hung down, the heart dangling over me.

I reached up and touched the charm, loving that he had the other side of my heart.

"God, I love you," he said.

My eyes widened.

He leaned back down and looked me right in the eyes. "So damn much."

Tears pooled in my eyes.

"I love your smile and your laugh and the way you know me. I know now I only need *you*, Aubrey. Only you."

My hand lifted to his cheek. He leaned into it. "You are the most frustrating guy I've ever met."

His brows shot up, unprepared for my response.

"But I have fallen so hard for you. And all I know is if you break my heart again, I'll—"

His lips captured mine, stealing away my words and my breath. This kiss was frantic and hot and I never wanted it to end. Kozart tugged at my shirt, somehow pulling it and my bra off of me. He reached down and pushed my jeans and panties down my legs as I pushed at his. He helped, pulling his boxers and shorts down the rest of the way. He crawled over me. "Tell me you love me," he said.

My hands drifted over his biceps, breathing him in.

"Say it."

I smirked, knowing I needed him to work for it.

He shook his head, both amused and frustrated by my need to be difficult. "Fine." He reached between my legs and his fingers found the wetness there. He chuckled. "Your body's talking for you."

"What's it saying?"

"It's saying you missed the feel of me on top of you." His fingers drifted over my folds.

Oh, God.

"And it's saying you missed me touching your body." His fingers pushed inside me.

Ahhhh.

"And it's saying you want me inside you all night long." His thumb circled my clit.

Gahhhhh.

"Am I right?" he asked.

"Don't stop."

He chuckled as he somehow produced a condom and rolled it on. "I'm not stopping. I'm just getting warmed up." He shifted his hips, positioning himself so his erection moved between my thighs.

I closed my eyes, ready to take him.

"No, no, no," he said.

My eyes opened.

"I want you looking at me." He rolled his hips and thrust inside me.

My back arched off the bed, my breasts pressing to his chest.

"Say it," he urged as he slowly pushed in and out of me.

I gnawed on my bottom lip as my eyes remained riveted on his.

"What's stopping you?"

I closed my eyes.

"Open your eyes," he said as his thrusts became faster.

My eyes opened just as his mouth returned to mine, his kiss deliberate and desperate. Was I making him that way? My hands slipped to his ass, my fingernails digging in as his thrusts became deeper. I loved the feel of him pounding inside of me. My breathing became ragged as the sensation between my thighs intensified. My legs began to tremble. He continued thrusting until I screamed his name and my body unraveled, glorious tremors shooting out to every part of me.

He followed me over the edge a minute later, dropping all his weight onto me. We lay there dragging in unsteady breaths for a long time.

He pulled back and his eyes searched mine. "Say it."

"I think I'm gonna close my dating profile."

He quirked a brow. "Why's that?"

"Because I love *you*, Kozart."

The elation of him finally hearing me say it swept across his features and a smile spread across his face. He leaned down and kissed me hard. "I knew it."

My forehead wrinkled. "You knew it?"

"There's no way this kind of love could be one-sided." He pressed his lips to my smile, kissing me for a long, long time.

And he was right.

There was no way only one person could feel this much love.

EPILOGUE

Eight Months Later

Kozart

I finished our newest song, "Sleepless," to the explosive applause of the South African crowd. They may have been excited about our new music, but I was excited about the next part of the show—my favorite part.

I looked to my right and out walked the most stunning brunette on the planet carrying a bottle of whiskey—my sponsors' whiskey of course—and wearing a torn Savage Beasts T-shirt, barely-there cutoffs, the cowboy boots I'd bought her, and her necklace.

My smile stretched wide as the men in the audience howled. I understood their reactions. And I couldn't blame them one bit.

Aubrey smirked, purposely swaying her ass as she walked across the stage, delivering the bottle of whiskey to me like she did every night.

Having her on the road for our summer tour had been just what I needed. Even Brielle and BJ had warmed up to the idea, noting how girls actually liked knowing someone had tamed the untamable Z Savage. Aubrey even had her own fan base now. Go figure.

I took the bottle from her, grabbing her hand before she could disappear. Her eyes widened, knowing this wasn't part of the act. Night after night she delivered me my whiskey, and night after night, I'd say something about how hot she was before she left me to my bottle and the remainder of the show.

But not tonight.

"How about a round of applause for my girl!" I shouted to the sold-out crowd of nearly one-hundred thousand.

The crowd erupted.

"Ain't she beautiful?" I said.

Aubrey tipped her head, obviously embarrassed by my question. It was one thing to comment on her as she walked offstage. It was another to have her stand there and have to endure the attention.

"She's smart, too. She just graduated with a degree in speech pathology. And she'll be starting on her master's degree in September."

The crowd cheered for her accomplishments.

"But the best thing about her," I told them. "Is that she's all mine."

Aubrey smirked, her embarrassment morphing to amusement.

"And I'm hoping to hold onto her for the rest of my life."

Aubrey

Time seemed to stall as Kozart took my other hand, his eyes never wavering from mine.

What was he doing? This wasn't part of the show.

"Aubrey," he said, a slight twitching in the corners of his lips. "I love you."

I nodded, unable to do anything else as my heartbeat knocked against the wall of my chest.

He lowered himself down—not onto one knee, but onto both knees.

My mouth fell open. The screams from the crowd were strangely drowned out by the sound of my heart pounding in my ears.

"I want to make you a promise," he said, his words reverberating throughout the massive outdoor stadium. "One I should've made the first day I met you."

Oh my God.

"I promise to love you and only you until the day I die."

I sucked in a sharp breath. Was this really happening? Right here?

"I promise to give you lots of country singing babies if you'll let me."

Nervous laughter burst out of me.

"I promise to spend every day trusting *you* and your love for me."

Tears welled in my eyes.

"Marry me, Aubrey. Make all my memories good ones and all my dreams come true."

I stared down at him on his knees before me, his eyes so hopeful—so full of love.

We'd met almost a year ago to the day. And since then, it had been a roller coaster of emotions. Both good and bad. But I knew with much certainty that Kozart Savage was it for me. I think I knew it the moment he took me to my sister's wedding.

I drew a deep breath and did the only thing I could in that moment. I nodded.

"I'm gonna need to hear you say it," he said with a smirk.

"Yes, Kozart. I'll marry you."

He jumped up, sweeping me off my feet and kissing me in front of nearly one-hundred thousand screaming fans. When he pulled away, he was smiling. "Shit. I forgot the ring." He lowered me to my feet and dug into the pocket of his cargo shorts, pulling out a beautiful diamond ring. "Let's make this official." He grabbed my left hand, and I extended my ring finger. He slipped it on and we both gazed down at the massive diamond before our eyes lifted to each other.

"I'll always fight for you, Kozart. Because you deserve that."

Tears glazed his eyes as he leaned forward and kissed me again.

The band began their next song, and I took that as my cue to duck away. Kozart wouldn't let me go though, so I turned to the crowd and waved to them, flashing my new ring.

The crowd erupted, and I shook my head amused, ecstatic, and so in love.

How could his team ever think these people wouldn't be happy for Kozart? How could they ever think this guy who'd spent so much of his life alone, needed to stay that way?

He had me now.

And I wasn't going anywhere.

THE END

OTHER TITLES

If you enjoyed Aubrey and Kozart's story,
check out the *For You* standalone series:
Book #1 *For Finlay*
Book #2 *For Forester*
Book #3 *For Crosby*
Book #4 *For Emery*

Until Alex
Since Drew
Before Hadley

CONTACT INFO

Facebook:/jnathanauthor
Twitter: @Jnathanbooks
Goodreads: jnathan
Instagram: jnathanauthor
Pinterest:/jnathanbooks
Website: Jnathan.net

ACKNOWLEDGEMENTS

Thank you so much for taking the time to read Kozart and Aubrey's story. I hope you enjoyed it as much as I enjoyed writing my first rock star romance!

To all the bloggers and readers who read and share my books. Thank you so much! I could not do this without you!

To my wonderful beta readers: Dali, Megan, Renee, Kim, and Heather. Thank you!! I always know I can count on you to give it to me straight.

To my editor Stephanie Elliot. Thank you for always being there for me and always making me give it my best. Even when you're tough on me, I know it only makes me and the story better.

To Gemma at Gem's Precise Proofreads. Thank you for your keen eye in finding those little mistakes I overlook. I'm so glad I found you. Thank you for loving their story!

To my PA Renee. Thank you for being you! I know I can always count on you for honest feedback and many laughs.

To Tiffany at T.E. Black Designs for creating a beautiful cover for me. I'm sorry I was so indecisive. But Kaz is so gorgeous. We needed to do him justice! LOL!

And last, but certainly not least, to my family. Thank you for all of your support and for being my biggest fans. I would not be who I am without you.

ABOUT THE AUTHOR

J. Nathan resides on the east coast with her husband and nine-year-old son. She is an avid reader of all things romance. Happy endings are a must. Alpha males with chips on their shoulders are an added bonus. When she's not curled up with a good book, she can be found spending time with family and friends, at soccer and baseball games, and working on her next novel.